BLOOD AND GAMES

**Lock Down Publications and Ca$h
Presents**
Blood and Games
A Novel by *King Dream*

Blood and Games

Lock Down Publications
Po Box 944
Stockbridge, Ga 30281

Visit our website @
www.lockdownpublications.com

Copyright 2023 by King Dream
Blood and Games

Lock Down Publications
Like our page on Facebook: Lock Down Publications @
www.facebook.com/lockdownpublications.ldp
Book interior design by: **Shawn Walker**
Edited by: **Jill Alicea**

Stay Connected with Us!

Text **LOCKDOWN** to 22828 to stay up-to-date with new releases, sneak peaks, contests and more...

Thank you.

Submission Guideline.

Submit the first three chapters of your completed manuscript to ldpsubmissions@gmail.com, subject line: Your book's title. The manuscript must be in a .doc file and sent as an attachment. Document should be in Times New Roman, double spaced and in size 12 font. Also, provide your synopsis and full contact information. If sending multiple submissions, they must each be in a separate email.

Have a story but no way to send it electronically? You can still submit to LDP/Ca$h Presents. Send in the first three chapters, written or typed, of your completed manuscript to:

LDP: Submissions Dept
Po Box 944
Stockbridge, Ga 30281

DO NOT send original manuscript. Must be a duplicate.

Provide your synopsis and a cover letter containing your full contact information.

Thanks for considering LDP and Ca$h Presents.

King Dream

CHAPTER 1

Kush smoke filled his lungs as Boss sat behind the wheel of his Cadillac Deville. He watched the scene that played outside of his car. Tricks pulled up to whores with their dicks in one hand and cash in the other. Whores hopped in and out of cars as they made their nightly quarters. Pimps walked up and down the strip, sweating the heels of fresh bitches.

A tap on his window disturbed the show for him. He rolled down his window to a sexy redbone in a white tank top and pink miniskirt so short that her butt cheeks hung out. She handed him a small fold of bills. Boss counted out $60.

"Bitch, you been out here four hours and all you got is $60?"

"Shit's slow out here."

"Bitch, you got to be shitting me. This track is live. I've been watching hoes less qualified than you hopping in and out of more cars than a valet parker. So Cherry, I know you got to be stroking game on me."

"You think I'm playing?" Cherry lifted up her shirt and bra, exposing her firm breasts and succulent nipples. "Look, Boss, I have nothing. And here, you can check my purse too!" She handed him her purse. She stood there with her arms folded across her chest, making popping sounds with the gum in her mouth. Boss rummaged through her purse. Finding nothing more than lose coins, condoms, makeup, body spray, baby wipes, gum, and her cell phone, he tossed it back to her.

"Get yo' ass back out there and get my money, Cherry. And I bet' not catch you out here bullshitting. You understand me?"

"Yeah, yeah, whatever." She rolled her eyes and walked off and Boss pulled off into traffic.

He had only had Cherry for two weeks. And at only 22 years old, she already been through more pimps than she could count. That didn't matter to him. He was hoeless before her and in desperate need of a hoe to pimp on. The chump change she brought him every night wasn't nearly enough to sustain them, let alone fulfill his dreams of getting to the top. Boss found no satisfaction with her production, but gladly accepted every bit she brought in. He figured any bitch with a hand in was better than a bitch with a hand out.

His phone rang. It was his right-hand man, Polo.

"Hello."

"My man Boss Bandz. What it do, my nigga?"

"You know me, fam. I'm just trying to get rich off a bitch."

"If that's what it is, then the news I got might be music to your ears."

"Oh yeah? Well, spit me that melody."

"You remember that chick Peaches I met last week at the gas station?"

"You talking about the li'l sexy caramel skin shorty with the blue Audi?"

"Yeah, her. Her and a friend of hers will be at the Rave tomorrow night for thirsty Thursdays. They want us to come kick with them. And dig, these ain't no broke hoes either. They say it's VIP all the way, and it's all on them. And get this: Peaches says her buddy is just as bad as her and gets money. I know you wouldn't want to miss out on a opportunity to check that out. So I hope your schedule is open for tomorrow night."

"Since you put it like that, then I guess I can make room. Count me in." Boss ended the call.

Boss and Polo had been more like brothers than best friends. Polo admired the pimp game, but never had a pimp bone in his body. He loved pussy too much to sell it. He was a hood nigga that sold weed and worked as a barber. But he and Boss were always tight as two mice in a cat fight.

***

The line to get in Club Rave stretched around the corner. As usual, everyone and they mama was trying to get in the club. Polo and Boss bypassed the line and went straight for the door. Their entrance was immediately blocked by a musclehead bouncer with a bad attitude. "Get to the back of the line!" The bouncer pointed towards the end of the line.

"Look here, my man, there's some ladies in VIP expecting us," Boss tried to explain.

The bouncer looked Boss and Polo once over with disgust as he quickly evaluated their wardrobe and lack of wealth. "Sure there is. As they say, there is someone for everyone, sir. You know what? I'm going to let the two of you in."

"That's what I'm talking about." Boss and Polo tried to walk past, but again were stopped.

"As soon as you get your asses to the back of the line and the line reaches you morons!"

"Who the hell you getting loud with, you thickhead bastard?" Polo walked up on the bouncer, but was quickly pushed back by Boss.

"Chill out, bro. Just call Peaches and tell her we out front and to meet us at the door."

Polo mugged the bouncer, then stepped to the side to call Peaches.

A few minutes later, Peaches appeared at the door. "Hey Polo!" She came out and gave him a hug. "What up, Boss?"

"Trying to get inside."

"Well, come on, the club is jumping." She hooked her arms onto theirs and walked to the door with Boss on one side of her and Polo on the other. "Rodney, these fellas are with me."

The bouncer smiled and shook his head at them. "Y'all fellas enjoy y'all night." Rodney held open the door for them.

Polo mean mugged the bouncer before walking in.

Once inside, they were greeted with the sounds of Wale and Jeremih's song "On Chill". It was theme night at the club. The club was set up with a heaven and hell theme. The main floor was hell. The waitresses wore small, tight red dresses with devil tails on their asses and pointy devil ears on their heads. The bartenders on this level were dressed like devils too. A staircase lead to pearly white gates where the VIP area was. The VIP had a heaven theme consisting of shiny gold-colored floors and white fluffy fur-like table cloths and booth seats. The waitresses and bartenders in this area dressed in angel costumes. The waitresses wore small, tight white dresses, rosy red cheeks, and angel wings.

They got to their area of VIP, and their table was adorned with bottles of Rosé, Hennessey, Ciroc, Remy Martin and Bacardi 151.

"Y'all help yourselves to whatever you want to drink. And if you don't see nothing you like on the table, then I'll tell the waitress to bring you whatever you desire," Peaches told them as they all sat down. She noticed Boss looking around uneasily. "Is something wrong, Boss?"

"Not that I find being in the company of you unpleasant or anything, Peaches. But I was under the impression that we would be joining you and a friend. I mean, was I misinformed?"

"Nah, you wasn't misinformed. My girl Isis is running a little late. But trust me, she'll be here. Matter of fact, there she go right there." Peaches pointed to the front entrance of the club.

Boss's eyes followed the point of her finger to its intended target. His eyes could've jumped out his head at the sight before him. The 5'8" Brazilian and Black mixed bombshell sashayed into the club with her long wavy black hair and olive skin tone. She made her way to their section in the VIP.

"Sorry I'm late everyone." Isis exchanged hugs and kisses on the cheek with Peaches.

"It's cool. We were just getting settled in ourselves. Let me introduce everyone. Isis, this is my new friend Polo, and this is his homeboy Boss Bandz." Peaches passed Isis a drink as Boss and Polo exchanged greetings with Isis.

Seeing her close up and those pretty green eyes of hers, Boss couldn't help but to let his eyes worship her beauty. She was thick in all the right places. To many men, she was the shit wet dreams were made of. Even Boss thought so himself, but he knew better to let her in on such thoughts.

Peaches and Polo excused themselves and made their way to the dancefloor. Not shy by far, Boss wasted no time taking full advantage of their time alone as he slid closer to Isis. Their conversation flowed smoothly as they quickly got to know each other. Then Boss asked a question that caught her off guard.

"Let me ask you something, Isis."

"Ask away." Isis looked at him with smiling eyes as she stirred her drink.

"What profession are you in that affords you to live as flamboyantly as you do?"

Isis was hoping that particular question wouldn't arise. She was enjoying Boss's company and getting to know him. She felt her answer to his question would steer his thoughts of her into a whole new direction. But she figured honesty would be the best policy.

"Honestly, honey, I sell pussy." Isis stared Boss in the eyes trying to catch his every reaction to what she just told him. To her surprise he remained unfazed. "Does that intimidate you or turn you off to hear that a bitch as bad as me spreads her legs and opens her mouth wide for different guys so that she could live this good?" She took a sip of her drink without breaking eye contact with him. Little did Isis know she was exactly the kind of bitch Boss was looking for. With Cherry being a lame horse in his stable, he knew if he were to get a bitch like Isis on his team, he could really start making his mark in the game.

"Actually, quite contrary to your assumption, I love whores because it was a whore who brought me into this world. In fact, a whore is the only kind of woman I can respect."

Isis furrowed her eyebrows, giving off a quizzical look to his unexpected response. "Really? And why is that?" Curiosity was killing her to know.

Boss couldn't help but to smile inside. He knew he had her complete interest and attention, and he planned to manipulate it in every way possible. "Because a square bitch don't know how to truly love. You see, a square bitch is nothing without a 9 to 5. Without a square job, she won't survive. She would allow her family to live on the streets eating out of dumpsters before she ever sells her ass. But a whore...oh baby, a whore's love runs deep. A whore eliminates all possibilities of poverty for her family. She humps day and night to keep her man with the latest Cadillacs and minks on his back. So to simplify my answer, baby, only a whore could love me and only a whore could I, in some strange way, love back." Judging by the smile on her face that she'd been so desperately trying to hold back, Boss knew his answer had impressed her.

"And what is it that you do for a living?" Isis was now even more curious about him.

Boss took a sip of his drink, set it down, then looked her deep in the eyes. "I'm a pimp."

Isis stared at him for a second with a blank face before busting out laughing. "You so silly. For real, what do you do?" Boss's facial expression didn't change. Isis noticed he was not laughing with her. "Wait a minute. You serious, aren't you?" She then recognized it wasn't a joke.

"Why? Does that intimidate you or turn you off that I make a living off of whores who spread their legs and open their mouths wide for different guys so I can live like I do?" Boss retorted back to her.

Isis smiled at how he hit her with the reverse. "Oh, so you going to use my lines against me, huh?" Boss gave her a conning smile as he took another sip of his drink. "Okay, no, I'm not intimidated or turned off by pimps. Because only a pimp could understand a hoe. Any more questions?"

"Yeah, I got another one for you. Are you truly happy with the pimp you got?"

Isis's face frowned up. "You do know not every hoe in the game has a pimp."

"Yeah, but you do."

"And how do you figure that?"

"Because it would be a crime against the nature of any pimp not to have a horse like you in his stable. And judging by your jewels and VIP lifestyle, you're too flashy and bold to be renegade. You're a walking lick for a stick-up kid. That not only lets me know you have a man, but also that he's a well-respected pimp in the game. So who is he?" Boss took another sip of his drink without taking his eyes off hers.

"I see you are very observant. To answer your question, I'm with Pimping Rome. I'm his bottom bitch. Being in the game, as you say you are, I'm sure you heard of him"

Boss could see the pride swell up in her chest as she mention her title as the bottom bitch of Rome. "I can't say his name rings any bells for me."

Isis shot him a strange look. "Seriously? You pimping and you don't know who Rome is?"

Boss shook his head no. "But I'll say one thing. He has to be one brave nigga to leave a hoe like you in the presence of a nigga like me."

"Is that right?"

"Indeed it is." Boss, feeling the moment, moved in closer.

Isis closed her eyes and leaned in until their lips almost touched. Before their lips could meet, the moment was quickly shattered as the sounds of Lloyd's song, "Feels So Right", began to flow through the speakers. Isis's eyes opened and she leaned away from him.

"This is my song. Come dance with me." Not waiting for his response, she grabbed his hand and they made their way to the dance floor.

On the dance floor, Isis slowly grinded her ass on him. Matching her rhythm for rhythm, he put his arms around her waist and whispered in her ear, "You know you broke a lot of rules in the game tonight. Surely you must be ready to choose up. Just pop that purse to me, and I'll give that nigga the call that will set you free."

"Cute. But trust me, I'm not breaking any rules Rome don't know about. And I know you don't think a few clever lines you spit to me will get me to leave Rome, do you?"

"Nah, but maybe this might help." Boss kissed her neck and let his hands cruise the curves of her body.

Immediately, chills shot up her spine. "Ooh, don't do that." Boss sucked on her neck. She moaned and ran her hand down the length of his manhood. "Damn!" she whispered, impressed by the size of it.

He turned her towards him. They swayed to the beat as he kissed her lips. Her breathing became heavy as his hand slid slowly up her skirt. Between her inner thighs, he could feel the heat and juices emanating from her love box. His fingers caressed her through her panties. She sucked his neck as he squeezed her ass.

The circles his fingers drew around her pearl tongue made her want to rip off his clothes and fuck him right there on the dance floor. He slid her panties to the side and bathed his fingers in her juices. She moaned in his ear as he pushed her closer to the edge of an orgasm. Feeling the liquor and herself a finger stroke away from cumming, she tilted her head back, readying herself to ride out her orgasm in complete bliss. But before she could reach that release, Boss's fingers pulled out of her paradise and ended her stimulation.

"Oh my God, why you stop?" She was panting like a lioness that had just chased down a gazelle.

Boss rubbed his soaking wet fingers on her soft, gorgeous lips. Then he slipped them into her mouth and she gladly sucked all her juices off of them. "The song is over, baby."

Isis looked around the club. Realizing where she was at, she quickly regained her composure. "Let's go back to our table." Isis straightened her clothes and followed Boss's lead back to the table.

Before they could sit down, Peaches rushed over.

"Isis! What the hell? I've been all over the club looking for you!" The sense of urgency in Peaches's voice gave Isis worry.

"We were on the dance floor. Why, what's wrong?"

"Rome called me looking for you! And he doesn't sound like he's in a good mood either."

"What did you tell him?" Isis quickly retrieved her cell phone from her purse. She found out she had missed nine calls from Rome while she was on the dance floor with Boss.

"I didn't have to tell him shit. He already knew where we were. He said if you ain't outside in five minutes, he's coming in."

"And how long ago was that?" Peaches checked the time of his call on her phone.

"Three minutes ago." Isis's eyes got big and she frantically raced to get her things together.

"Boss, it was nice meeting you. I'm sorry to have to rush off like this, but I'm sure you can understand my need to hurry." She kissed him on the cheek and exited the gates of heaven.

Boss couldn't let her get away from him like that. Not when he felt he was so close to getting her. He quickly chased behind her catching up with her at the bottom of the stairs. "Hold up baby."

"Boss, I have to go now or Rome going to fuck me up!" Isis turned to continue leaving.

Boss grabbed her by the arms and turned her back around to him. "Listen, baby, the chemistry we displayed tonight is too strong to be abandoned. Your life could be better than this if you leave with me."

"But am I supposed to do about Rome?"

"Just pop that purse open and choose up, and I'll end those worries." Isis paused a second, looked around the club, then started to open her purse.

Before she could pull out any money, a hand grabbed her by the back of the neck. "Bitch, those ovaries of yours must've turned into a pair of balls. Because I'm sure you got my message, and you still made me have to come in and get you?" The tall, muscular, brown-skinned man with a bald head put so much fear in Isis, her eyes wanted to pop out her head.

"Rome, daddy, I was on my way out now."

Polo and Peaches walked up to join the scene.

"I don't want to hear no excuses. Why you ain't out there getting my money?"

"Rome, business was slow on her end. So I invited her to come out with me and catch some tricks here at the club."

Rome turned to Peaches. "Shut up, bitch! I didn't ask yo' ass to be this hoe's advocate. So speak when you spoken to."

Peaches pursed her lips. Polo, feeling the need to come to his date's rescue, quickly intervened.

"Hold on, you big John Coffee, Green Mile-looking mothafucka. You check yo' bitch all you want, but you better watch yo' mouth when it comes to mines."

"Or what?" Rome said as he released his grip on Isis and walked up on Polo.

Boss quickly cut in between them. The music stopped and the whole club watched the drama unfold.

"Dig this, P. That hoe right there is ready to choose up and leave with me. So you can get yo' paws off my property."

Rome looked Boss up and down then laughed at him. "And just who the hell you supposed to be, nigga ? Captain save a hoe ? Because you damn sho' ain't no pimp."

"Nigga, I'm Boss Bandz! A true pimp! I don't save no hoe."

The frown on Boss's face made Rome smile. Knowing it didn't take much to tap into the young stud's emotions, Rome decided to play on his like he did with a bitch. He turned to the crowd.

"Y'all mothafuckas hear this shit? This nigga here says he's a pimp. Have you ever in yo' lives ever seen a pimp dressed like this?" Rome pointed to Boss's wardrobe. "This nigga look like a JCPenney's model." The crowd erupted into laughter. Boss glowed red with anger and embarrassment as Rome continued his storm of insults. "You say you a pimp? Then put your money where your mouth is and prove your game." Rome pulled out a roll of hundred dollar bills and slammed it on a nearby table. "There's three G's says you can't knock that bitch. That should be easy money for you since you say the hoe was going to choose up to you anyway."

Boss knew he could barely cover that kind of bet if he lost. That was all the money he had to his name. But he had no worries of losing. He knew after the way he had Isis on the dance floor he had her in the bag without a doubt.

"Bet it up then."

"Cool. Game on, young stud."

All eyes were on Boss as he walked over to Isis. Isis stood there shaking and scared with her head down.

"Look here, baby. We both know you aren't happy with that nigga you with, and with me is where you belong. So shake loose that leash and come get hooked on me." Isis made what sounded like sobbing noises as her shoulders jerked up and down as if she was crying uncontrollably. Boss put his hand on her chin and lifted her face up towards him. He then found out she wasn't crying.

Isis burst out in laughter. "Shake loose that leash and come get hooked on me? Oh my fucking God, I've now heard it all. You actually thought I would leave Rome to be with you? Nigga, I'm

Queen Isis. I would never leave my throne to be with a peasant."
Isis turned to Rome. "Daddy, this nigga call himself pimping and
didn't even know who you were." Isis turned to Rome.

Rome shook his head. "I should be clutching my pearls at such
lack of acknowledgement for the king. That's right, youngling.
Bound and crowned, I'm the king pimp of this here game. Can't a
nigga alive who call himself pimping say he haven't heard of me.
But I guess it wouldn't hurt to overlook the lack of recognition from
a nobody-ass nigga like you. Now let's get down to business. It
seems you failed to knock me for the bitch, so make like a good
whore and pay a pimp."

Polo was just as pissed as Boss was at the disrespect and hu-
miliation Rome poured upon him. He whispered in Boss's ear. "I
got my noodle knocker on me, my nigga. Just say the word, and I'll
be more than happy to blow this nigga's top back."

Boss shook his head no. "Go to the car, Polo, and grab that
dough out the speakers."

"Yeah, be a good puppy and go fetch my paper. And don't come
back with any surprises either." Rome pulled a 44 Magnum out his
waistband and set it on the table next to him.

"Boss, let me——"

Boss held up his hand, cutting Polo short. "Polo, just go get the
money!"

Polo mugged Rome as he walked off." Boss knew Polo was
down to put Rome in a box if he gave him the word. He was as loyal
as they came. But Polo was a hothead who didn't always think
things through before he acted. Boss was sure Polo didn't see
Rome's goons lurking in the shadows. More than likely, they were
packing heat too. An oversight like that could've cost them their
lives if they were to handle the situation the way Polo wanted to.

Polo returned and reached into his waistband. But before he
could pull anything out, three goons came out the shadows of the
crowd with pistols drawn. Rome had his 44 in hand, ready for action.

Polo froze in his tracks. "Hold up! I'm just grabbing the
money!" Polo slowly pulled out the roll of cash from his waistband

and held it up for all to see. "You see? Now how about y'all boys put them slingshots away before somebody gets hurt."

Rome nodded to his goons and they all put their guns away.

Polo tossed the money to Boss. Boss stared at the roll of bills a second in disbelief at how he had lost his entire small savings. He had to rack up quickly before hard times came around. Because at this moment, if Cherry was to get jammed up by the cops, he wouldn't even have enough dough to bail her out. He got his arm ready to toss Rome the money, but Rome stopped him in his tracks.

"Hold up! Somebody teach this young nigga proper etiquette. I am the king, boy! You don't throw my money to me. You serve it to me with respect!" Rome said to further humiliate him in front of everyone.

Peaches and Isis laughed uncontrollably as Boss reluctantly walked over to Rome and put the money in his hand. "Now that's a good boy." Rome had the smile of a wicked Cheshire cat on his face.

"Come on, Peaches, let's roll." Polo held out his hand. Peaches walked towards him.

"Syke!" She change directions and dipped over to Rome. She stood on one side of Rome and Isis stood on the other.

"Sorry, Charlie, but these hoes belong to me." The VIP server approached Rome with the night's bill. "Dig, baby, tonight's fun was on these studs. Give them that bill." Rome walked past the server and made his exit out of the club with Isis and Peaches in tow. The server handed Boss the tab. The tab read $1200. He reluctantly gave the server a credit card.

After getting his credit card and receipt, Boss rushed out the door. He watched as Rome slid money in the hand of the bouncer who gave him and Polo trouble earlier getting in. Rome hopped into a red Mercedes AMG and pulled off with Isis behind him in a silver convertible BMW and Peaches in her blue Audi. Polo came out of the club with all the bottles of liquor that had adorned their table in VIP. Boss looked down at the bottles in his hand, then looked at him.

"What? If we have to pay for all this shit, you damn right we taking it with us." Polo carried the arms full of liquor to the car.

Boss watched the taillights of Rome's and the girls' cars disappear down the road. The embarrassment they caused him was shameful. He wanted revenge. But more than anything, he wanted the power Rome had.

King Dream

CHAPTER 2

The next morning, Boss arrived at Perkins diner. He took a seat in front of an older, well-dressed gentleman who sat reading the newspaper with a steaming hot cup of coffee. The man spoke to him without taking his face out the paper.

"Boss Bandz. What you need from an old P like me, youngblood?"

"Big Hunnid, you speak as if me in your presence is something out of the ordinary. Can a nephew come enjoy a nice breakfast and conversation with his favorite uncle?"

Big Hunnid put down the paper. "You ain't slicker than oil, Boss. I know you want something. So if you going to run game on me like one of these whores, you could at least buy me breakfast first."

They both laughed.

"I can do that." Boss waved the waitress over and they placed their orders.

Fifteen minutes later, she returned with their orders. Their meals of grits, scrambled eggs with cheese, sausage, bacon, and toast looked picture perfect. After a little small talk and catching up on the latest events in life, Boss got right down to business.

"I want to ask you something, Unc."

"I figured that much. Go 'head." Big Hunnid buttered his toast and seasoned his eggs with salt and pepper.

"What can you tell me about this pimp they call Rome?"

Before Big Hunnid could take another bite of his eggs, he was frozen by Boss's question. "Why do you want to know about Rome?"

"Why the concern and hesitation, old timer?"

Big Hunnid dropped his fork on his plate and exhaled. "Because you're speaking of bad news. The man you speak of is known to be the greatest pimp in the game. That son of a bitch drove many hoes and pimps alike to suicide and the insane asylum. So I ask again, why do you want to know about Rome?"

Boss poured two packs of sugar into his coffee and stirred it as he spoke. "Polo met this bitch a few weeks ago named Peaches. We met up with her and a friend of hers name Isis last night at Club Rave."

"Peaches and Isis! Nigga, have you lost your damn mind? Them hoes are thoroughbreds. If you think for one minute that elementary game of yours is gonna work on them bitches, think again. Them hoes will chew yo' yellow ass up and spit you out."

"Well damn, thanks for the boost of confidence."

"I'm just keeping it real with you, youngblood. Your game ain't ready to be played on that playground. And I would hate for you to end up like those other jokers. Rome ain't nobody you want to fuck with. He's a nigga without a soul. The man pimped out his own mammy and beat her ass every time she came short on his bread. That bitch Isis you talking about is his bottom bitch. And that bitch is just as heartless as he is." Big Hunnid pushed his plate to the side and sparked up a cigarette.

"I hear you. But I got to get back at him and that hoe. It's personal."

"What you mean get back at them?"

Boss broke down last night's events to him. Big Hunnid shook his head at the shame of it all.

"Boss, you fell for the Charlie game. The oldest trick in the pimp's book. A pimp sends his hoe out to catch the attention of another pimp. She makes him think she's gonna choose him. Then her pimp shows up and challenges the stud for the bitch and loses all his bread. They call it the Charlie game because back in the day, it was a hip saying that came from a tuna fish commercial that went 'Sorry Charlie' when shit didn't go as planned. So pimps started calling it the Charlie game. The best thing you can do, youngblood, is to take the lesson as a blessing and count your losses, baby. Because I'm telling you, Rome and that bitch ain't the kind of people you want to get in bed with." Big Hunnid took a long pull of his cigarette.

"I get what you saying, OG, but this nigga and his bitch tested my game, and the pimp in me refuses to let it go. Now I'm not afraid of Rome or any nigga at all. I see you don't have faith in me and you ain't got to believe in me. I'm going to show you and everyone else in the game that I, Boss mothafuckin' Bandz, will be the greatest pimp to ever walk this earth. Thanks for the conversation, pimp. Breakfast is on me." Boss got up and dropped some money on the table.

Big Hunnid smashed out his cigarette butt in an ashtray, then grabbed Boss's wrist before he could walk away. "Wait a minute. Youngblood, this bitch got you under her spell already and you don't even know it yet. I see there's no way I can talk you out of going after this bitch and challenging Rome for the throne." Boss gave his uncle a look of wonder. "Yeah, I know it's not just a revenge thing you have with Rome. You want that crown. Your heart yearns for that throne. And my silly ass is going to help you the best way I can by laying these jewels on you. Before you can take on Rome, you got to get yo' shit together, you dig?"

"What you mean?"

"What I mean is, one horse in the stable won't win this race. Build your stable up with some of the baddest bitches you can find. And you work them hoes like a Mexican in an Asian sweatshop. Then go challenge these small-time pimps and out-game them. Earn their respect and work your way up the ladder. Your name got to start ringing bells if you want to get Rome's attention. You dig?"

"Dig. Now that's a plan I can follow through with, old timer."

Boss left the diner, then swung by the hood and picked Polo up to renew his license. Music filled the silence in the car since neither one of them wanted to discuss last night's events, and last night was all either of them could think about.

They got to the DMV and found the place was packed, as usual. Everyone was trying to address their motor vehicle needs before the weekend. Boss took a seat while Polo waited in line. Pissed as he was, more so at himself for falling for the Charlie game, Boss decided to look Isis up on Facebook. After scrolling through all the people named Isis whose pages appeared before hers, he finally found the one he was looking for. He checked out the pictures on her page. *Damn, this bitch is fine!* he thought to himself. As he continued scrolling through her photos, he came across a pic of her standing between two white girls and Peaches squatting in front of her. A blonde stood on her left and a brunette on her right. They posed in front of Rome's AMG with him behind the wheel in a tailored pink Armani suit.

Boss noticed the indicator said that Isis was currently online. He decided to send her a DM. "A round of applause to you, bitch. You pulled that weak-ass Charlie game on a pimp. That shit was child's play. If you really want to impress me, you got to come better than that..."

Isis immediately messaged back. "Baby, if you want to talk game, then you need to get yours up. Because if you can fall for game as weak as that, than you are not ready for me. I mean, did you really think you was going to knock me with some weak-ass lines and a good finger fuck? Like, I told you I'm Queen Isis. The baddest bitch in the game, and every true pimp knows my name. You know how many top-notch pimps try to get me in their stables on a daily? But there ain't no nigga out here with more game than Rome. And I'm a loyal hoe with concrete feet. Like a car with no gas, baby, I ain't going nowhere. But it's always a pleasure to see niggas like you try to get me..." She ended the message with a series of smiley faces and laughing emojis.

Boss wanted to message her back and give the hoe a piece of his mind, but thought against it. It would be foolish to expose his emotions to the hoe. He got up to go talk to Polo.

"Drew, get over here!" a woman yelled. But her words weren't enough to stop what was about to happen. Before Boss could react, SPLASH! A little boy ran into him, spilling grape soda all over his jeans.

"Damn it, Drew! Now look what you've done. I am so sorry, sir. You can send me the cleaner's bill."

Boss wiped the soda off with his hand the best he could. "No need. I got——" He looked up and stopped in mid-sentence when he saw the woman's face. "Queenie?"

A sudden smile of realization took over her face when she noticed that the man she was apologizing to was Boss. "Boss?" She ran into his arms and hugged him as tight as she could. "I haven't seen you in forever! How have you been?"

"I been alright. Look like you're not doing too bad yourself. You back in town to visit?"

"No. I moved back here a couple of months ago after my grandmother passed."

"Oh, I'm sorry to hear that. I see you still looking good as ever though."

"What, you thought these good looks would fade away once out of your presence?"

"Never know. But who's the lucky stud that got you to have his baby?"

Queenie gave him a look of total confusion. "A baby?" Boss looked down at Drew and her eyes followed. "Oh, Drew's not mines. He's my nephew."

"Nephew? That's Tina's son?"

"Yup."

"Little square-ass Tina who used to always quote the Bible and pray for our sins when she would catch us playing hide-and-go-get-it?"

"Yup, that's her. She's not the same Tina you remember. But anyways, Drew's daycare was closed today, so I'm watching him until Tina gets off work."

"So no kids? No man?"

"I have more important things in life to worry about."

"Like what?"

Rhythm of their conversation got cut short when Polo approached the scene. "Can you believe this shit? No matter how good you look, they still manage to take a messed-up picture to put on your license." Polo held up his license.

Drew tugged on Queenie's arm. "Tee Tee, McDonalds!" Drew whined to her.

"Okay, Drew, we're going. Boss, I got to go feed him. Take my number down and call me."

"Nah, you take mines." He spat his number to her and she programmed it number in her phone.

"When you want me to call you?"

"When you find yourself not able to have one single thought without me being a part of it."

"And what if that never happens?"

Boss kissed her behind the ear. She smiled at how he still remembered her sweet spot.

"Then it wasn't meant to be." He turned and walked away.

He couldn't help but think to himself how good she looked. She looked even better now than she did when they were teenagers with her long blonde dyed hair, gray eyes, and sexy yellow skin covered in tattoos. Even though her beauty was unquestionable back then, she now seemed to break the limits on beauty and master the art of gorgeous - a masterpiece he had to get back in his possession.

Once back in the car ,Polo began unloading his questions about Queenie. "Yo, who was baby girl in there you was talking to?"

"That was Queenie. We grew up together. First love type shit, you know." Boss spoke nonchalantly and shrugged his shoulders.

"So why y'all cut ties?"

Boss looked over at Polo. "She was also my first hoe."

Polo's eyes grew big enough to burst out of his skull. "That bad-ass foreign-looking bitch in there used to sell pussy for you?"

"When we were 16, right before I met you, her mama found out I was pimping her out and sent her to go live with her grandma in Elk River, Minnesota."

"And you didn't try to keep in touch with her? Call her? Text her? Skype her? Email her? Mail a letter? Or even send the bitch a message in a bottle? Nigga, you tripping."

"You don't understand. Her grandma was real strict. She was one of those Holy Bible-thumping Jesus thugs. That woman didn't play no games. Queenie wasn't allowed to talk to boys or so much as look their way too long or her grandma would beat her ass in the name of Jesus. You feel me?"

"Yeah, I know the type. My Aunt Jeanie used to soak a belt in blessed oil and read us Bible scriptures before she whooped our asses. She said something about sparing the rod and casting out demons or some shit. But anyways, go on."

Boss shot Polo a weird look before continuing. "Anyways, I tried to contact her a few times throughout the first year she moved. But whenever I called, her grandma would pick up the phone and chew me out telling me not to call her house anymore. She intercepted all my letters and Queenie wasn't allowed to have a cellphone or a computer. So after a while, I quit trying."

Polo nodded his head. "That's some sad Romeo and Juliet type shit. You okay? You need a hug?" Polo jokingly opened his arms to hug Boss. "Come on, bring it in."

Boss shook his head and laughed at him.

What I want to know is, what is shorty mixed with?"

"Her pops was Italian and Black, and her mom was Creole."

"Goddamn! She even sounds as good as she looks. You think she still sells pussy? Because I'll pay for some of that."

Boss shook his head and drove off.

King Dream

CHAPTER 3

Saturday morning, Boss stopped by his mama's house. As he pulled in front of her house, Aaron, a.k.a. Chief Hicks, was walking out of the house and to his squad car. Aaron was the chief of police and had been a friend of the family for as long as Boss could remember. He was sweet on Boss's mama and always stopped by every chance he got, trying to woo her into marriage, but Boss's mama wasn't interested.

Boss got out of the car and greeted Aaron with a handshake. "What it do, Chief?"

"Headed back down to the station to earn my pension. You been keeping your nose clean?"

"Always."

"Good. But you know if you ever need me, let me know."

"I'll do that."

"Alright, I'll catch you later." Aaron got in the car.

Boss gave have him a lazy salute then headed in house.

Walking through the door, he was greeted with the delicious aroma of bacon, eggs, pancakes, and the sweet melodic voice of Mary J. Blige singing her song "Feel Like A Woman". He found his mama in the kitchen standing over the stove, scrambling eggs and singing along with the music. He couldn't help but be amazed at how after the hard life she'd had, she still looked young enough that people thought she was his sister and not his mother. She had a 5'8" 135 lb. frame, high yellow skin tone, and long wavy red hair and gray eyes, thanks to her mama being Irish and her daddy Black. Pimps still saw dollar signs when they saw her. But when Boss saw her, he saw the only woman in the world he would go to heaven or hell for. Tweety no longer danced or walked the track, but she still kept a black book of johns she saw on a regular. And as long as she'd been in the game, the only pimp she'd ever had was Boss's father, Cadillac Bandz. He was killed when Boss was a kid. As much as Tweety missed Big Bandz, she didn't talk about him much. Anytime Boss brought his name up, she'd tell him to let the dead rest as they should.

"Boy, are you going to just stand there and watch me, or are you going to give your mama some sugar?"

"I see you still have those eyes in the back of your head." Boss went over and gave her a kiss on the cheek.

"A mother doesn't lose such a talent. Now spark up that blunt on the table before we eat. And tell me what's been going on with you." Tweety scooped eggs onto their plates.

Boss leaned against the counter and sparked up the blunt.

"I've just been having the damndest time trying to get Cherry to step her game up."

"Boy, you can't expect that hoe to step her game up if you don't step yours up."

"What you mean?"

"Look at it like this. A pimp is like a hoe's coach. And that hoe is only going to play as hard as her pimp pushes her."

Boss sat down at the table. "So what should I do?"

Tweety walked over and placed their plates on the table. She took the blunt from Boss and sat down before answering his question. "You got to stand on that bitch. Show her you ain't playing and that your word is law. Put your foot so far up that bitch's ass she'll shit Nike symbols to stay in check."

"I ain't much of a woman beater. You taught me to be more finesse than gorilla."

She rolled her eyes at his lack of comprehension.

"Boss, you don't have to beat a bitch with your fist to get an understanding. But sometimes words being played on the strings of a hoe's emotions aren't enough. Sometimes a hoe needs that physical touch."

"So you suggesting I sex her good to get her to act right? Because I do that."

Tweety slapped him upside the head. "No, fool! You don't reward a dog for pissing on the carpet. So why reward a whore with loving when she hasn't earned it? Which brings me to another thing. Keep your dick out these bitches before they get the wrong idea about their position in your life. What I'm suggesting you do is find a way to put the fear of God in that hoe so she will think twice before she ever tries to bullshit you." She passed him the blunt after blowing a thin cloud of smoke out of her mouth. Tweety had always been straightforward and blunt with Boss and raised him to be the same way with her. There was never anything the two of them couldn't talk to each other about, and that made their bond that much stronger.

"I feel you. After the other night, it's no doubt I need to step my game up."

"What happened the other night?" She wondered what was the latest news in his life.

"Me and Polo went to Club Rave last night and got Charlied."

Her faced frowned up and she punched Boss in the chest. "You let some bitch Charlie you?"

He gave her the rundown of last night's events and told her about the Facebook messages between him and Isis.

"Now I know you probably itching to get back at her, but never chase a bitch, because then you'll be playing her game. And in her game, she's got the control. Play the hoe and not her game. Make her chase you. I know her type. Hoes like that, you have to prove yourself to be the greatest. You have to show her that you are greater than the nigga she worships if you want her to bow to you." Tweety got up to pour them something to drink. "So who is this pimp she's with?"

"Some ole skool cat."

"Oh yeah? What's his name? I know all the old heads in the game. Let's see…we got Tony Swag, Pimping Ball, Drop top Lou, Daddy Lac——"

Boss cut her off. "Nah, this some nigga named Rome."

At the sound of his name, she dropped the glasses of orange juice, shattering glass all over the kitchen floor.

Boss rushed over to help her. "You alright, Ma?"

"I'm okay. I guess I must be high as the clouds to be so clumsy. That was some good weed." She put on a fake laugh to disguise what she was really feeling.

"Yes, it was," Boss agreed as he helped her pick up the broken pieces of glass.

"You know, Boss, now that I think about it, maybe you should just forget about this Isis girl and her pimp."

Just then, Boss realized it wasn't the weed that made his mama clumsy. He knew then that she knew something about Rome that scared even her. It filled him with anger knowing there was a nigga alive who could put such a fear in his mother.

"You know that nigga, don't you?" Tweety remained silent and continued picking up the broken glass. "Mama, answer me."

"Boss, leave it alone."

"Leave it alone? Why the fuck is everybody so afraid of this nigga?" Boss started ranting.

She gripped his arm. "Just trust me, Boss! Stay away from him! Nothing good can come from it."

Boss looked down and notices her hand was bleeding from a piece of glass she was unaware she was squeezing. "Ma, you bleeding!" She looked down at her hand.

"Shit!" She released the piece of glass, then put her hand to her mouth and sucked on the cut.

"Here, let me see." Boss snatched a wet towel off the sink and wrapped it around her hand. He sat her down at the table, then cleaned up the remaining mess.

Feeling it was time Boss knew the truth, she called him to the table. "Boss, come sit with me." He complied with her request. "It's a lot you don't know. A lot of secrets I tried to leave buried with your father."

"Ma, you never kept anything from me a day in your life. So what could be so bad that you would have to keep it a secret from me?"

It was going to take a little more weed to tell Boss what she had to tell him. She picked up a fresh blunt and put it between her lips. Boss reached over and lit it for her. She took a long, hard pull and held it in a second before blowing it out.

"Your father was king pimp before Rome was. Rome was your father's right-hand man. They were like brothers. Rome got his game from your dad. When Rome started pimping, he had a girl who he fell hard for. She was feeling him too until she found out that he wasn't the true author of the game he was spilling on her. That same game she fell in love with. She found out the true man behind the game was your father, Cadillac Bandz. One day, she took all the money she'd been cuffing from Rome and went to the Bird House bar where all the pimps hung out and chose up to Cadillac in front of Rome and all the other pimps. Your father didn't want to do it to Rome. But he knew he wouldn't be respecting the game if he didn't, and all the other pimps and whores would lose respect for him. Being king pimp, he couldn't afford to disrespect the game like that." Tweety paused to take a few more hits of the blunt before passing it to Boss.

"So what he do?"

"He did the only thing he could do. He accepted her. Of course, him and Rome fell out behind it. Rome swore Cadillac snaked him for her. For that, he vowed revenge on Cadillac. After that, Rome sold his soul to the devil and became one heartless son of a bitch. He started poisoning pimp's whores and setting pimps up with murder charges. He worked his way up the ranks, trying to become king pimp. But his game was never a match for your father's. No matter what Rome did, Cadillac was always ten steps ahead of him, and Rome hated that. Your father's pimping was flawless. But your father's only sin in the game is what got him killed. Being king pimp, he knew he had to do something about Rome. His sin was that he felt guilty for taking away a woman Rome loved. Your father's love for Rome kept him from killing him when he knew he should've. Instead of killing him, Cadillac banished him from the game. And with tears in his eyes, he told Rome if he ever seen him again, he would be forced to separate his soul from his body."

Boss inhaled a cloud of smoke into his nose and passed her the blunt. "And then what?"

Tweety dumped the blunt ashes off in the ashtray, then continued. "Rome disappeared for a while. Then one late night, your father got a call. He said he would be back, that he had meet someone at docks. But he never returned. They found his boat in the middle of the lake blown to pieces. The current was so bad they never found his body. Then that very same week, Rome returned to take the crown."

"Are you telling me this nigga is the one responsible for my father's death?"

"That's what everyone believes. And Rome never denied it. But still, of course, no one can prove it."

"This nigga calls himself a pimp and beefs with Pops over some punk-ass bitch?" Boss ranted on.

Tweety slammed her uninjured hand on the table. "That bitch was me! I was the one who left Rome for your father."

Shock rippled across Boss's face. "What? Hell no. You playing with me, right? You said Pops was the only pimp you ever had. Now you trying to tell me this nigga Rome is the one who turned you out?"

"First off, Rome didn't turn me out. I was hoeing long before I met Rome. I said your dad was the only pimp I had because all the game and connects Rome used belonged to your father. Rome was nothing more than an extension of Cadillac. Every time I broke bread with Rome, he would break bread with Cadillac for giving him game. So it was never Rome pimping me. He was just a middleman. Your father was my real pimp."

Boss stood up put his hands on his head and paced the floor. "I don't even know what to do with all this. Why you never told me none of this before?"

Tweety got up and made Boss turn to face her. "I didn't tell you because I didn't want you to feel the need to take the throne from Rome. I didn't want you to get wrapped up in all of this. I lost your father already. You are all I got left, and I don't want to lose you too. But now as I look into your eyes, I can see there's no way I can keep you from doing exactly what it is I don't want you to do. So wait here. I got something for you." She went off to her bedroom.

Boss's mind raced as he stood there in the kitchen. It felt as if his head was ready to explode. He couldn't believe the same nigga who embarrassed him at the club the other night was the same nigga who pimped his mama and hated his father for taking her. Now Boss not only wanted to dethrone Rome; he wanted destroy him completely.

Boss braced himself on the kitchen counter as Tweety walked back in the kitchen holding a large black book. "Your grandfather wanted your father to be a doctor or a lawyer or something socially respectable. But I swear it was as if sometimes that man could see into the future. He knew Cadillac would want to follow in his footsteps and all the risk he would face in the game, and he wanted him to be prepared for it. He wanted him to take over the throne. He used to say the throne belongs to the Bandz family. So to ensure your father and his descendants' success in the game, he wrote what he called The Holy Bible Of Game." She handed the book to him. He flipped through it as she spoke. "I was waiting for Rome to die before I ever gave this to you. I didn't want you going up against such a monster. Seeing you're gonna do it anyway, I'd rather you to be prepared. Use it to take back the throne. Just watch your back for Rome. He's the snake that even the devil has to keep an eye on."

Boss knew exactly what she meant. He saw the snake in Rome the night he met him. But it didn't scare him. It made him want to go after him that much more.

King Dream

CHAPTER 4

After leaving his mother's house, Boss's mind swarmed with so many thoughts. Answers were given to questions that he never thought he would have to ask, but this understanding he now had was well overdue. He went home, flopped down on the couch, and cracked open The Holy Bible Of Game.

The first page read like a letter from his grandfather Big Daddy Bandz to Boss's father Cadillac. The page read:

Dear Cadillac,

If you're reading this, then that means you have made it to the throne. I want you understand what's in you cannot be denied. What's in you is the blood of a long line of pimp gods. And this bible I have written for you and your descendants will give y'all all the knowledge and guidance needed to maintain the throne and be the pimp gods y'all are. This game is my heart and most sacred passion. I seen the pimp in you when you were just a baby and I knew you would share the same passion I do for the game. The throne is important, son. It's important, because as pimp gods, it's our responsibility to ensure this game is respected and played right by all. The absence of order breeds chaos. It is the responsibility of the one who holds the throne to ensure order. The throne cannot fall into the hands of the wrong man. My only request is that you maintain the throne by all means and respect the game. But I'ma tell you, this game ain't easy. Hard times will come and tough decisions would have to be made. Some friends will become enemies and some enemies will become friends. Just remember, respect the game and its laws and you will always make the right decision. Even when it feels like you didn't. A pimp god gives his life to the game. We are the sacrificial lambs. Take these jewels, son, and rule the game. And know I will always be watching.

Love always,
Your father,
Big Daddy Bandz

Boss turned the page and began reading. Intrigued by the wisdom in each line, he was immediately drawn into the book. His mind became sucked into it like a vacuum. He studied the book until he fell asleep.

He awakened the next morning on the couch with the Holy Bible of Game laying open on his chest. He put the book away and jumped in the shower. His mind was spinning with all the things he learned about the game overnight, things he should've known but didn't, and things no man could ever know unless he was a god in the game. He couldn't help but notice all the sins he had committed in the game. Just then and there, he vowed to never be such a sinner again.

***

Later that night, Boss picked up Polo and they drove to the hoe stroll on the south side so he could check up on Cherry.

"So this big black-ass bitch came in the barber shop, right. I'm talking about this bitch looked like Biggie Smalls in a muumuu. She had two little girls with her – well, I shouldn't say little. These bitches was like eight and ten years old and looked like linebackers for the Tennessee Titans. They come in the barbershop with chicken grease and crumbs on their mouths talking about where Daryl at?"

Polo was telling Boss a funny story that happened at the barber shop that day, but Boss's mind was elsewhere. All he could think about was how he had to get his shit together. And to do so, he had to start making some real changes. To start getting the type of bread he needed, he had to first get Cherry to step her game up.

As they pulled up on the track, Cherry came running up to the car, tapping on the window. Boss rolled down the window and Cherry tossed him a small fold of bills. Boss counted out $75. He wanted to bury his foot in her ass. "Where's the rest of my money, Cherry?" he asked without even looking her way.

"That's all I got, Boss, damn! It's slow out here."

Boss turned his head towards her and narrowed his eyes as he looked dead into hers with the grimmest mug she had ever seen. Feeling like he was seeing right through her, she looked away. She was right. Boss could see she was lying.

"Bitch, stop playing with me and give me my mothafuckin' paper. And if I got to get out this car to get it, you might as well tell me now who to ship your worthless-ass body to."

"Daddy, I gave you all my money. What you got is all I have. You know I wouldn't play you."

Boss was starting to lose his patience with the bitch. The lies she kept spitting out her cocksucker was making his blood boil. And now her opportunity to come correct without severe consequences had expired. He unlocked the car doors.

Cherry got nervous, but she stuck to her story. "Look, baby, I don't have anything." She tried her normal routine of lifting her bra and giving him her purse.

But this time, Boss wasn't going for none of it. "I guess you're one of those dumb bitches that don't believe my threats are real until you feel it. Well, hoe, I'm going to make you a believer." He opened the door and stepped out of the car.

Cherry was stunned and stepped back with the intent to run, but Boss grabbed her in one swift motion and bent her over the hood of the car.

"Daddy, please, I don't have any more money."

Pimps and hoes on the track observed from a distance.

Boss put his hand between her legs and stuck them up her pussy. She cried out and her coochie made a suction sound as he pulled out a roll of bills. He flipped her over and looked into her eyes with his grim mug while holding up the roll of money dripping with her juices. Cherry braced herself for an ass whooping she knew she deserved.

"Boss, I can explain."

"Explain? What is there to explain? Get in." He hit the button on his keypad, popping the trunk.

"Boss, don't. Please don't make me get in there," Cherry pleaded.

But her pleas went unheard as Boss snatched her purse and cell phone, then pushed her into the trunk and slammed it shut. He casually walked around to the driver side door.

An ole skool pimp with a long gray perm and green and gold suit yelled over to him. "That's right, young pimp. You trunk that hoe and get her mind right. Keep real pimping alive, baby!" The old player smiled at Boss and took a pull of his cigarette.

Boss nodded his head and got in the car.

Polo looked over at Boss. "Damn, nigga, you kidnapping your hoes now? What you finna do with her?"

Boss shot him a wicked smile, then turned up the subwoofers to drown out Cherry's pleading and crying.

***

Boss drove forty minutes outside the city to a secluded wooded area. He popped the trunk, snatching Cherry out and putting her over his shoulder. "Polo, grab that bag and shovel out the trunk."

Polo grabbed the items slammed the trunk closed, then followed Boss into the woods. Cherry pleaded with Boss not to kill her, but Boss continued walking without saying a word to her, which scared her even more.

It was so dark out in the woods that Boss and Polo had to get the flashlights out of the bag to see their way through. After walking almost a quarter of a mile into the dark woods, they finally found a spot Boss was satisfied with. He threw Cherry down. She hit the ground with a heavy thud.

"Polo, dig a grave for this bitch."

Without any questions, Polo grabbed the shovel and began digging.

"Stand up, bitch, and take them clothes off," Boss ordered her.

Cherry sat up and slowly scooted away from him. With much fear and tears in her eyes, she realized she truly underestimated him. "Please, daddy, don't. I'll do anything. Just don't kill me," she pleaded.

"I'm not going to repeat myself."

The look in his eyes showed her there was no way of talking herself out of whatever he had in store for her. She nervously and reluctantly complied with his orders, stripping off all her clothes until she stood there naked as the day she was born. He put a strip of duct tape across her mouth, then took a blindfold out of the bag and put it over her eyes. He tied her hands to a branch high enough to leave her feet dangling in the air. Her heart pounded harder as she realized then and there she wasn't going to make it out of those woods alive and that no one would care that she was missing.

"That hole deep enough, Polo."

Polo dropped the shovel and dusted off his hands. "Damn, I didn't know it would be so much work digging a grave. The shit look easy in the movies."

Boss picked up three tree switches and braided them together, making them stronger. "Cherry, when you steal from me, you hurt me, baby. So now you must feel my pain."

He swung the switch like a slave master's whip, landing it square on her plump red rump. Her body squirmed in midair. She cried out in agony, but her screams were muffled by the tape across her mouth.

Boss tossed Polo the roll of bills he took out of Cherry's twat. "Add that up."

Polo counted it, then sniffed it. "Smells just like pussy." He sucked his fingers. "Taste like it too," he joked.

But Boss wasn't in the mood for laughs. "Polo! How much?"

"Damn, my bad. It's $300 here."

"Then that's 299 more licks to go."

She mumbled something incomprehensible. No doubt she was pleading for mercy. But Boss had none for her as he brought down the switch on her bare ass over and over until she received the 299 more licks she was promised.

He took out his handkerchief and wiped the sweat from his forehead. "Polo, spark up a blunt and let's roll."

"What about her?" Polo pointed at Cherry, who was hanging from the tree with blood running down her legs.

Boss looked over at her and shrugged his shoulders. "What about her? Leave that hoe hanging. I'm sure with that blood dripping down her legs, the wolves will be here soon. They'll take care of her ass."

Cherry squirmed and mumbled as she heard Boss and Polo's footsteps leaving away.

They got back to the car. Boss slipped an 8-ball & MJG's CD in. The song "Pimp Hard" played. Polo puffed on the blunt and at the same time, stared over at Boss strangely. Boss sat there swimming through his thoughts until he noticed Polo's eyes on him. "What?"

"Shit, my nigga, you tell me. You constipated? Need some fiber in your diet or something? Yo' ass been space jamming all day and walking around with a mug. What's really good, my nig?" He passed the blunt to Boss.

Boss sucked in a hard pull of the kush, holding it in his lungs a few moments before slowly releasing it through his nostrils. "Just a lot of shit been on a nigga's mind since the other night at the club."

Polo waved him off before cutting in. "Man, don't sweat that shit. Mothafuckas will forget all about that mess in due time and find another cat to laugh at."

"I don't give a shit about none of that. I'm actually glad that shit happened, because it showed me if I want to be taken serious in this game, I have to start taking this game serious. If I'm going to take Rome off the throne, then I'm going to have to pimp hard. And that's just what I'm going to do."

"You coming for Rome that way, huh? Smart. Take the nigga's crown and make his bitch ass bow down. I can dig that. But what about the bitch Cherry? You going to leave her there hanging?"

"Nah."

"You going to kill the bitch?" Polo leaned in and whispered.

"I should. But no. I just wanted to scare the hoe enough so she would think twice before she ever tried to play me. We'll go get her after we blow another blunt."

Polo remained quiet for a second then turned to Boss. "So you telling me I dug a grave for nothing?"

"It wasn't for nothing. It was a psychological stunt. I wanted to play on her mental so she would really think I was going to kill her."

"Psychological stunt? Yeah, me and that bitch both going to need therapy. You know how hard it was to dig that grave? And now you ain't even going to put nobody in it? You better go kill a deer, squirrel, rabbit or something and put it in there. Look at my damn hands. I have callouses. Callouses, Boss! I'm a damn barber. What the hell I'm doing with callouses on my hands? I tell you what. Let me kill the bitch and I'll find you another one."

Boss couldn't help but laugh at him as he ranted on about digging a false grave.

"Stop crying and smoke so we can go get this bitch."

Boss handed him the blunt, then gazed out into the woods as the music played.

King Dream

CHAPTER 5

Boss pulled up to his house and popped the trunk. He wrapped his jacket around Cherry's nude body and carried her into the house. He laid her on the bed. She winced and whimpered as he cleaned the welts across her bottom. Cherry stared at the wall with tears running down her cheeks. Boss desired to know her every thought right then.

"Cherry, baby, why you want daddy to hate you? Life can be so much sweeter for the both of us if you let me love you?"

Without looking away from the wall, Cherry answered him. "I don't want you to hate me, daddy." Then, in a tone barely audible, she said, "I'm just scared."

"Did you say you scared?" She nodded her head yes. "With a nigga like me in your life, what could you possibly be scared of?"

This time Cherry turned over and looked him in the eyes to address his question. "You. You make it so easy for a bitch like me to fall in love with you. And it scares the shit out of me. It scares me because every man I ever loved played with my heart. They left me high and dry without a dime to my name and nowhere to go but to the next nigga. I didn't want to go through that again. I wanted to be prepared this time. So if you were to leave me, I would have a little money to live on and wouldn't have to run to another man just to get by."

Boss could see for the first time the bitch was being truthful. And to him it explained the reason why at such a young age she been through so many pimps. He sat down on the bed next to her. Cherry sat up and stared into his eyes as he spoke.

"I understand, baby. But that's where trust and belief come in at. You got to believe in me like a Christian believes in Jesus and a Muslim believes in Allah for this to work. And trust that as long as you are faithful to me with your purse and loyal to the respect and honor of my name, I will always care for you and never leave you without. If you want the best of me, baby, then you got to give me all of you. So hoe, can you promise me that love and trust that I so demand?"

She nodded her head. Then she reached in her hoe bag and pulled out a spray can of Oil Sheen. Boss watched her as she removed the bottom of the can and rolls of money came sliding out. She gave it all to Boss. Boss counted the bread and couldn't believe how much money she'd been cuffing from him.

"Yes, daddy, I promise. For here on out, I will give you my all. Just please, baby, don't do me bad like the other men I gave my heart to did." She wrapped her arms around him and squeezed tight as more tears rolled down her cheeks.

"Never give me a reason to and I won't."

They stretched out on the bed and he held her as they both fell asleep.

***

Boss awakened early the next morning to an empty bed and Cherry nowhere to be found. He called her phone and got no answer. *Damn, did I go too hard on the bitch last night and run her off?* he thought to himself. If she ran off, he could live with that. But if she went to the police with those lashes and bruises on her, he knew they would put him under the jail. With no money for a good lawyer, that was something he couldn't afford to happen. He quickly got dressed to go and search for her. But before he could even tie his shoelaces, Cherry came through the door with bags in hand.

"Bitch, where the fuck you been? I've been calling your phone and you ain't answer. I was getting ready to comb these streets for yo' ass."

"Daddy, don't be mad. I had two dates this morning and I didn't want to wake you. I know I missed your call. I couldn't get to the phone in time with all these damn bags in my hands. And I was only a few blocks away when you called. I made $500 and stopped and got you breakfast."

Boss snatched the money out of her hand. "Next time, hoe, leave a note or something. I thought I was going to have to take you back to the woods for good this time."

Cherry sat the bags down and walked over to Boss. She wrapped her arms around his neck and gazed into his eyes. "Daddy, you don't have to worry about having any more problems out of me. I'm going to give my all to making you rich. I made you a promise. And like a good hoe that's true to her word, I'm going to keep that promise."

Boss knew a hoe's word didn't mean shit. But the faith he now had in his game would ensure that hoe's word was kept.

She showed him all the clothes and shoes she had one of her tricks buy for them. He planted a kiss on her forehead.

"Now that's a hoe I can be proud to call mines."

Boss thought back to what his mama told him about not rewarding a hoe with loving if she didn't earn it. The bitch finally pissed outside and not on the carpet, so he might as well reward her. He then turned Cherry around and bent her over the couch. He lifted up her skirt and snatched off her panties, then pulled her ponytail as he slid deep off inside her. Her whimpers turned into moans and her moans into screams as he thrust in and out of her relentlessly. Her nails clawed into the headrest of the couch and she screamed his name in victory as she reached her orgasm. Boss pulled out of her without achieving his own climax.

Cherry turned around, weak and out of breath. "Baby, you didn't get yours. You want me to give you some top?" She was willing to do whatever to make him feel as good as he just made her feel.

"I'm good. This wasn't about me getting off. This pleasure was all yours. You give me mines every time you come correct with my money."

She smiled up at him with a look of satisfaction. Boss knew exactly what Cherry needed. She didn't need to be made love to. She needed him to thug her guts out. And by the smile on her face and the shake in her legs, he could tell he gave it to her just the way she wanted it.

"Listen, you won't be working the strip club this weekend as we originally planned. Those marks on your ass need to heal. Put some more A&D and Witch Hazel on it. I'm going to get you a room and have you work the internet."

"Okay, daddy." Boss slapped her on the ass. Cherry whimpered. "Ouch, daddy!" She gave him a playful pouty face.

"You li'l freak, you know you like that shit. Now get yo' ass in there and warm up my food."

She walked out of the room switching her ass. She looked back at him with a smile on her face, blew him a kiss, then sashayed into the kitchen.

***

Boss and Polo conversed as they drove around the city running errands. Boss had one more stop to make before heading over to the hotel he had Cherry posted up at. They got to their destination, New Deal Auto, a car lot off Appleton Street. They hopped out and looked around at the cars available.

"Yeah, Polo, that bitch Cherry finally getting with the program and stepping her game up."

"Of course she did. I mean, you beat her ass like a slave that came up short on massa's cotton. Straight up, my nigga, that was like watching the movie *Roots*. You beat that bitch like the Jews beat Jesus. I ain't seen a beating like that since my aunt Jeanie caught my cousin Junior watching a porno."

"Something is seriously wrong with you."

***

After leaving the car lot, they arrived at Cherry's hotel room. Cherry was seated on the edge of the bed painting her toenails. When she saw Boss come through the door, she ran over to hug him.

"Hey, daddy. I missed you."

"Show me in cash just how much you missed me."

"I could make all the money in the world, Boss, and it still couldn't compare to how much I love you and be missing you. But I did good though."

"I'll be the judge of that. Go get my money."

Cherry got the stash of cash from under the nightstand and handed it over to Boss. She watched him with a swell of pride as he counted out $2800.

"Did I do good or what, daddy?"

"Yeah, bitch, you did good." Boss leaned against the dresser and slapped the money repeatedly against his palm and stared at Cherry.

"Then what's wrong?" Cherry began to feel nervous, hoping she didn't do anything to disappoint him.

Boss took a seat on the bed and patted his hand on his lap. "Come here, Cherry baby." Cherry walked over and rested her ass on his lap. Boss held up the stack of money in front of her face. "I'm going to need many more nights like this out of you. And it's going to take a team of bitches pushing that same effort to get to where we going."

"Daddy, if you suggesting we get more bitches, then I don't know about that one. You know I don't vibe with other hoes like that. Bitches be on some hating shit."

The nerve of this bitch, Boss thought to himself. "Bitch, you ain't got shit! What the fuck is there to hate on?" Boss snapped at her, causing her to nearly jump out her skin. He took a deep breath and continued what he was saying more calmly. "Look here, hoe, I'm going to the top with or without you. If you with me, then give me your all and leave that jealousy shit behind. Because you alone can't get us to where we're going." Tears began to flow down her face. "Now what you crying for?"

"Because I'm not good enough for you. So you need another girl. And soon you will be replacing me." She turned her head away from him before she could break down.

Boss took her face and turned it towards him. "Look here, baby, if you love me like you say you love me, then understand me. This is not about replacing you or you not being good enough. This is about the fight we have making it to the top. For this fight, baby, I need all the strength I can get. I'm going up against some real monsters in the game. And one finger can't make a fist. It's a lot of cats out here praying on our downfall. It's hoes out here that think you're washed up already. Pimps who say you ain't shit but a rabbit-ass hoe with no loyalty and quick to jump ship. But not me, baby. You see I believe in you. That's why I took the chance on giving you the privilege of being my hoe. I don't need you. You need me, and I want you to share this dream with me, and that's why you are here with me. Now are you going to help daddy build by any means necessary? Or are you going to help these haters out here destroy us by all means?"

Cherry wiped away her tears and weighed her options carefully in her head. She hated the idea of not being the only bitch in Boss's life. But she knew it was either share him or not have him at all.

"Boss, I love you and I'm with you all the way, daddy. And if you say to push these dreams into reality, it's going to take a team of us..." She paused a moment and swallowed back a sob. Then she held her head up with pride and continued speaking. "Then daddy, I'm going to be a team player."

Boss was breaking through the walls she put up and forcing her to surrender. To reward her cooperation, her placed a kiss on her lips. As Boss read in the Holy Bible of Game, a hoe will build walls around her heart to protect herself as she plays in the psyche of all men. Her goal is to make you fall in love with her and not her with you. It's her war tactic. But a real pimp is the master of mental warfare.

"Now you thinking like a true hoe of mines. It's time to start going hard out here, baby. So it's going to be some changes. From now on, you going to be going out of town majority of the time doing your thing. When you at home, you will be working the club and the internet. I will be too busy taking care of other business then to be playing your chauffeur. So I bought you a little something to get around in." Boss gave her a set of keys. Her face lit up.

"Boss, is this what I think this is?"

"Why don't you go outside and see."

She ran outside and hit the alarm on the keypad. A chirp came from a glossy forest green-colored 2015 Impala with tinted windows. She got in and started it up. Boss got in on the passenger's side and watched her excitement.

"You like it?"

"I love it! And it's all mines!" Then a sudden realization brought her back to reality and the excitement started to fade. "Well, I guess it's only mines until you get mad at me and take your car back. I been through that routine before."

"No, it's all yours, baby." Boss passed her the title with her name on it.

She was astounded. "No man has ever did anything like this for me before." She stared at the title in disbelief.

"I told you, just trust me, baby. I would never leave you high and dry. This ain't just about me. I want you to have what you want out of life as well. This is just the beginning of what's to come. I'm going to get you your own business and some properties. We going to take expensive vacations to exotic islands and fuck on the beach as the sun sets. We won't ever have to worry about shit. Can you picture that like I can, baby?"

"Hell yeah, daddy!"

Boss gave her another kiss on the lips. "But for that to be possible, we got to get to where we're going." He kissed her neck and her eyes rolled in the back of her head.

"Just tell me where to go and what to do and I will be there to get it done."

Boss held a smile of triumph on his face. He had finally broken the bitch in. Tweety had taught him early on that women are emotional creatures, and she taught him just how to play on those emotions. Cherry was no different from any other woman, and he had her right where he wanted her: in total submission. And now that his bottom bitch was in check, it was time to build his team.

King Dream

CHAPTER 6

His head fell back and he released a loud groan. Her head bobbed up and down. The slurping sounds she made as she sucked him sent him into a state of ecstasy. While one hand was wrapped around his member stroking him as she sucked, her other hand slipped into the pockets of his pants that rested around his ankles. She cuffed his bankroll as he got closer to his well-pursued release. She rolled the money under the bed just before he came.

"Ahhh! he groaned as he made his release. He pulled up his pants and thanked her for a good time, then left out the door without a clue that he had just been got. Cherry locked the door behind him and began packing as fast as she could. She wanted to be in the wind before the trick learned his bankroll was missing.

After checking out of her hotel room, she jumped in her car and made a call. "Hello?" the caller on the other end whispered.

"Bitch, you ready?"

"Yeah, I'm leaving out now. Meet me at the Check Cashers on Lamar Lane."

"I'll be there in fifteen minutes." Cherry hung up then said to herself, "Boss is going to be so pleased with me when I get home from Memphis. I got him a bad new Puerto Rican bitch and I made 4 G's. Yeah, I'm giving him my all. This nigga captured my heart and makes me feel like no other man has ever made me feel. I never fell this deep for someone before. I will give him anything he wants and do whatever he says no problem. But all hell is going to break loose if this nigga breaks my heart. I can't take another heartbreak. Especially one that will cut this deep." She looked at a picture of him that dangled from her rearview mirror. "I promise, Boss, if you fuck me over, you going to regret the day you met me." She kissed her two fingers and touched them to his picture, then drove off.

She pulled up to the Check Cashers on Lamar Lane. Macita came out with bags in hand, walking quickly to the car. Cherry pushed the button to open the trunk. Macita threw her bags in and quickly got into the passenger seat.

"Cherry, we got to get out of here now! I hit this nigga's safe and took everything. He's going to wake up any moment and notice I'm gone right along with all his shit. And that loco mothafucka will be stalking these streets looking for me!" Macita spoke so fast it was almost as she was speaking Spanish. Cherry could see she was nervous and scared. She could remember being just as scared the first time she ran from a pimp after breaking him off.

She pulled a .380 out her purse and laid it on her lap. Boss had bought her a gun so she would feel safe whenever she was out of his reach. She put the car in reverse but before she could pull out, a champagne-colored Cadillac pulled up, blocking her in. A short, dark-skinned man with dreads and a mouth full of gold stepped out.

Macita's heart almost jumped out of her chest. "Cherry, that's him! That's Memphis!"

Cherry clutched her heat. The tint on her car was dark enough that it would be hard for him to see in. She tossed Macita a jacket to cover up with just in case. Memphis walked past, eyeing Cherry's Impala, but kept stride straight into the Check Cashers. Not sure if anybody in the Check Cashers had seen Macita get in her car, Cherry decided to go in.

Memphis approached the teller. "Say mane, you seen a li'l Puerto Rican bitch bring her ass in here? A young pretty bitch carrying a bunch of bags?"

Cherry walked in before the man could answer. The teller looked in Cherry's direction and right then, she knew he knew Macita was with her. Cherry quickly intervened before the teller could give her away.

"You talking about that wavy-haired Puerto Rican girl with the big breasts?"

Memphis turned around, just noticing Cherry standing behind him. He adjusted the Cartier frames on his face as he checked her out. "Yeah, that's her. I'm a friend of her father's and he is worried sick about her. She ran off this morning after they had an argument. You seen her?" Memphis was lying through his teeth, but Cherry knew better.

"Really? Then why isn't her father here looking for her? I mean, you say he's the one concerned and all."

"We split up to search for her. He's out looking in other areas for her. Why you ask? You a friend of hers?"

"No, I don't know her. How old is she anyway?"

Memphis starting to get irritated by all her questions. He closed the gap between him and Cherry. "She's 18."

Cherry, not feeling a bit intimidated by him, looked him in the eyes as she spoke. "Well, it seems to me that by law, she's old enough to do without parental guidance."

"She's a li'l slow in the head and has special needs." He casually opened his jacket, exposing a 9mm. "So as you can see, it's a matter of life and death that I find her. So I ask you, please, have you seen her?"

Macita peeped through an opening in the jacket that covered her and saw Memphis approach Cherry. She watched intently as they conversed. "What could she be talking to him about? Why did she even go inside there? Is she working with Memphis on the low? Was all this a test?" So many questions plagued her mind as her nerves grew more and more uneasy by each passing second. She watched Memphis open his jacket and saw the gun on his hip. "Oh my God, is he going to shoot her in front of everyone?" Knowing how crazy Memphis was, her thoughts put nothing past him. She learned that the first week she met him. She watched him pistol whip one of his girls for sitting on his car and leaving a scratch. Then, while covered in blood and crying, he made the woman apologize to Brenda, which was the name he gave his Cadillac. Macita knew then she had run from one bad situation to another when she got with Memphis.

Cherry continued trying to get Memphis to leave and search elsewhere so they could get the hell out of there. "The girl you looking for came here just a minute ago. Looking all crazy and scared. She got in the car with some pretty boy-looking nigga in a black Lexus. They had just pulled off right before you pulled up."

Memphis looked over at the teller for conformation. Cherry peeked a $50 bill out her purse to show the teller.

"That's exactly what I was going to tell you. Where they're headed, I have no clue." the teller told Memphis.

Memphis, satisfied with their answers, walked out the door. Cherry slipped the teller the $50 bill she promised and left.

Memphis stopped at the rear driver's side door of Cherry's car as she got ready to get in. He turned to Cherry. "I hope my concerns for a friend didn't rub you the wrong way. I can get besides myself when it comes to people I hold dear to me. I would like to make it up to you. So how about you take down my number so we can arrange to do just that."

"Sorry, I'm happily married."

"With no ring on your finger?"

Cherry looked down at her hand. "Oh, it fell down the sink a few weeks ago and my husband hasn't let me live that down since." Slight movement from the passenger seat caused the car to shake just a little, but it was enough to catch Memphis's eye. He removed his Cartier frames and squinched his eyes, trying to see through the tint. "Well look I hope you find your friend. I got to get going. My husband doesn't like it when I'm late."

"Who that in the front seat?"

"That's my little sister. She's sleeping."

"Your little sister, huh?" Memphis sensed she was bullshitting him. He walked to the front of the car to get a better view through the front windshield. But before he could get a good look, police lights flashed and a quick scream of the squad car's siren caught both his and Cherry's attention. The squad car parked besides Memphis's precious Brenda. The officer stepped out the car.

"Whose car this is?" The officer had a strong southern drawl.

"That there car mines, officer," Memphis admitted.

"Well, I'm writing you a citation for illegal parking. Step on over here and let me see dem license."

"Um, Officer, could you please have him move his car first? I'm late for work."

"Sure thang, ma'am. Sir, park yo' vehicle off to the side over there."

Memphis gave Cherry a stern look, then complied with the officer's orders. Cherry hopped in her car and backed out. She uncovered Macita before stopping her car next to Memphis and the police officer. She rolled down her window.

"Thank you so much, Officer. I would hate to get the new girl here in trouble with our boss for being late because of me," Cherry told the officer while pointing to Macita, but looking at Memphis.

"No problem, ma'am. You ladies have a nice day."

"You too, Officer." Cherry rolled up the window and pulled off, jumping on the highway straight back to Milwaukee.

King Dream

CHAPTER 7

Boss and Polo walked into Burger King for a quick bite to eat. "Man, I'm hungrier than an Ethiopian houseguest." Polo rubbed his stomach while scanning the menu.

A young teenage girl with braces and bad acne stood behind the cash register. Boss approached the register first.

"Welcome to Burger King. May I take——"

"I'll take it from here, Sarah. Why don't you go man the drive thru for me?" the manager cut in. Catching a glimpse of Boss while working the drive thru window, she couldn't pass up the opportunity to be the woman at his service. "As she was saying, sir, welcome to Burger King. May I…take…your order?" The manager, a ghetto redheaded chubby white woman with a badly-tanned face covered in freckles, said seductively before smiling and displaying a mouth full of tarnished gold teeth.

"I'll take a number four with a Coke," Boss said while staring up at the menu and paying her no attention.

A tall, gorgeous, and thick dark-skinned woman walked up to the manager. "JoAnn, I'm finished unloading the truck. What do you need me to do next?"

The manager rolled her eyes and exhaled a deep breath. "Can't you see I'm with a customer? Why don't you go make some fries or something."

The woman ignored the manager's bad attitude and walked over to the fryer. Boss's eyes followed her the whole way.

"Damn, people can be so rude. I'm sorry about that, handsome, will that be all?"

"Nah, I'll take her too," Boss replied without taking his eyes off the woman at the fryer.

"Her?" JoAnn pointed at the woman on the fryer with a look of disgust on her face. The woman on the fryer looked over and noticed they were speaking about her. Her eyes locked onto Boss's and she couldn't resist giving him a shy smile. "Well, sorry, sir, she ain't on the menu. So is there anything else I can get you?" The manager now had an attitude with him.

"She didn't say she wasn't on the menu. And the last I checked, this was Burger King, and the motto is have it your way." Boss took his eyes off the manager and back on the woman frying French fries. "Say, chocolate, come here for a minute."

"She is at work. If you want to talk to her, you can come back when she's off the clock. Until then, there is no fraternizing with customers." The manager then turned her attention to the woman on the fryer. "And that's enough fries, Jessica. You can go to the back and do inventory," JoAnn ordered Jessica in an attempt to get her out of his eyesight. "Now sir, I have other customers waiting. So if that will be all, your total is $6.34." Boss paid her no attention and walked behind the counter. "You can't come back here!" Boss walked up to Jessica with swag in his step.

"Look here, baby, my name is Boss Bandz and besides beautiful, you are…?" Boss held out his hand for her to shake.

"Jessica." She shook his hand.

"Jessica, I need to ask you something, baby."

"What?"

"Don't you want more out of life?"

"Of course I do. That's why I work hard at my job. A job which you probably about to get me fired from."

"Then I'll be doing you the greatest favor of your life. Because baby, you been chasing your dream with the wrong king." Boss pointed to the cardboard advertisement for Burger King with its mascot king on it. "I know you tired of shaking fries and slanging pies. You need a pimp like me in your life to keep you right."

"A pimp? I've never sold my ass a day in my life." Jessica don't know if she should've been offended or flattered by his approach.

"Yeah, I know you haven't. You been giving it away to these cats out here that left you with nothing more than a wet ass, heartache, and a pillow full of tears. Get with me, baby, and I'll show you the value of that gold between your legs."

The flow of their conversation was interrupted when the manager started yelling at Jessica. "Get yo' ass back to work! Or you can head yo' ass down to the unemployment line." She then tapped Boss on the shoulder.

He reluctantly spun around. JoAnn stood there with her hands on her hips and a face full of attitude. The customers along with the employees who pretended to be working watched the drama unfold with excitement.

"You can either leave now, or I can call the Po-Po to escort you up out of here. I don't know who the hell you think you is…Bishop Don Magic Juan or somebody! Coming in here like you own the place and shit."

"Dig this, hoe, you talk to her like that or interrupt me one more time, and I'm going to slap yo' copper mouth ass so hard it's going to knock pounds off yo' chunky honky ass. You want to call the police, bitch, be my guest. But until they get here, I suggest for your own safety you take yo' ass back to work and out my face. Now excuse my back." Boss spun back around to Jessica.

The employees covered their mouths and looked the other way to conceal their laughter.

"I'm calling the cops!" Steaming pissed, JoAnn stormed off to the back office.

Jessica's mouth dropped. She was stunned at how Boss stood up to her boss, and the way he took up for her impressed her that much more.

"What's it going to be, baby? Because my time is extremely valuable and I don't want to waste it on a dreamer with no ambition to push those dreams into reality. I'm a rare breed, and this is a once in a lifetime opportunity for you to have a real pimp like me in your life. So you got til the time I leave out that door before this opportunity goes extinct." Boss turned his back to her and strolled towards the door.

Jessica stood there stuck, wondering what she should do, as JoAnn came out of the back office.

"You better leave. I called the cops and they're on their way."

As she continued ranting, Boss dug in his pocket, pulled out a box of Tic-Tacs, and tossed it to her.

"Chew the whole fucking bottle, you vile mouth horse breath bitch."

The whole restaurant erupted into laughter. JoAnn blew breath into her hand and smelled it. "What y'all laughing at? Get back to work!"

Before Boss hand could touch the door, Jessica was right there to open it for him.

"And what you think you're doing?" JoAnn asked her.

Jessica took off her Burger King hat and shirt and threw it at JoAnn. "Pushing dreams into reality." Then she and Boss walked out the door with JoAnn's insults bouncing off their backs.

"You'll be crawling back. They always come back. Next!" she yelled from behind the register.

Polo was next in line. "Check this out, baby. I love that little hood swag you got going on. And that brass smile of yours. Maybe you can hook me up with a number three and a strawberry shake, then we can go to that back office of yours and I'll show you a real Whopper."

JoAnn rolled her eyes at him. "Sarah, take his order!"

Sarah came to the register with her braces shining, exposing all the scrap metal in her mouth as she smiled. "Welcome to Burger King. May I take your order?"

Polo's face balled up at the sight of the hideous-looking girl. "You know what? I lost my appetite." He left the restaurant and rode out with Boss and Jessica.

***

Jessica came scrolling out of the bank after withdrawing all her savings. She returned to the car and handed Boss the whole three grand she had saved up. "There you go, daddy."

Boss counted the money then held it out for her to see. "Jessica, baby, this here is a small investment into a greater future for the both of us. Your whole life changes right now. In fact, even your name changes. From this moment on, you will be known as Coco."

"I like that."

"Of course you do, bitch, because I thought of it."

"Bitch?" Feeling disrespected, Coco leaned away from Boss and looked at him funny.

"Yeah…bitch, hoe. Get used to these names because they are my terminology of affection. Like when a coach yells and insults his players to bring out the best in them so they play hard enough to win the game. That's what it's like when I call you by such names. And not only that, you got to have thick skin in this game, Coco baby. Because mothafuckas out here will call you even worse names than that, and you can't let that shit shake you." Boss cuffed her chin in his hand and looked into her eyes. "Can you dig what I'm saying, bitch?"

She kissed him on the lips.

"I can dig it, daddy."

Boss glanced up at his rearview mirror and saw Polo was nodding his head to the rhythm of his and Jessica's conversation. That let him know Polo was soaking up game from the backseat. Boss chuckled and drove home.

Back at home, Boss was met at the door with Cherry's arms wrapped around him. "Oh daddy, I missed you!" She looked up and saw a woman standing behind Boss. "Daddy, who is that?" Boss seized Coco by the hand and pulled her in front of him.

"This is Coco, the newest member of our family. She's fresh to the game, so you make her feel at home and show her the ropes out there. You understand?"

Cherry quickly assessed the beautiful chocolate goddess for any blemishes. She needed to find a flaw with her so she could feel more secure about herself. So far, she found none.

"I got you, daddy." Cherry introduced herself to Coco with a hug. Then she put her attention back on Boss. "I made you four G's. It's on your dresser. And I got one more surprise for you?" Cherry hurried off to the back. She returned moments later with Macita. "This is Macita. I met her on the track in Memphis. She ran off from this nigga named Pimping Memphis. I couldn't let a pretty little thing like her run the streets alone, so I talked her into coming home with us."

Boss took Macita by the hand and twirled her around to get a good look at her. "Nice! You ready for some real pimping in yo' life bitch?"

"Being waiting for some ever since I been in the game."

"Then break bread like Jesus said."

Macita went off to the back room and came back with both hands full of money. Boss kept his cool, but inside he was jumping up and down with excitement as he counted twenty G's. "Macita, hoe, you know the way to a pimp's heart. Welcome to the family, baby." Boss opened his arms and wrapped them around her. He then embraced Cherry and whispered in her ear. "You did real good, bitch. And tonight, I'm going to show you just how proud I am of you."

That made Cherry feel happier than a dog receiving a pat on the head by its master for doing a good job. If she had a tail, it would've been wagging.

Boss turned to Macita. "Now give me that nigga Memphis's number." She complied and Boss dialed the number.

By the third ring, Memphis answered. "Who the fuck is this?"

"Well, today, pimp, I guess I'm the bearer of bad news for you. This is Boss Bandz, and I'm calling to let you know that hoe Macita told me she had dreams of being a star. I told her I was headed that way: outer space. So she abandoned yo' cruise ship and a boarded my spaceship. And as we speak, we're on our way to the Milky Way, baby."

"Fuck that bitch, mane! Keep that hoe! I just want the bread back she stole from me!"

Boss removed the phone from his ear and looked at it strange before speaking again. "You aren't really asking me to return the money, are you? Surely being an extraordinary gentleman of leisure, you understand that that's not going to happen. It's part of the game, baby. The spoils of war. You were slipping on your pimping and somehow let a hoe have too much access to your riches."

"I don't know who you is, nigga. Yo' name don't ring any bells in the church of this game."

"Then I guess your church forgot the god they worship. But you and the rest of your congregation will see real soon who I am and fall to y'all knees and worship me." Boss had said all he needed to say and ended the call. He glanced over at his women. "You hoes get naked. We're going to celebrate with a little fun."

The girls quickly came out their clothes. Cherry looked slyly over at Macita and saw she didn't have much of an ass, and that gave Cherry that superior feeling over her. She then glanced over at Coco and finally found a flaw on the chocolate goddess. Coco had a few burn scars on her back from a house fire when she was a kid. It wasn't anything too hideous, but it was enough to make Cherry feel like the baddest bitch in Boss's stable. And to Cherry, that's all that mattered.

King Dream

CHAPTER 8

Boss's hoes had been humping like desert camels, getting his money. His game had been elevating to extraordinary levels, and everyone around could see it. It was all thanks to the Holy Bible Of Game.

Things might've been looking up for Boss, but for Cherry ,it was a whole 'nother story. Her own obsession with being the best girl in his stable had her feeling the pressure of trying to compete with Macita and Coco.

She sat at the bar, sipping her drink. One of the other dancers, a white strawberry blonde woman with large breast implants, approached her.

"Cherry, girl, you look like you're on your last leg out there. What's wrong, hon?"

"Sugar, I am beat. I've been up all night grinding. Then I had four dates today before coming in. I just don't have the energy tonight." Cherry could barely keep her eyes open. She was in desperate need of rest.

"Well, if you want, I got something that could help with that."

"Like what?"

Sugar pulled a small baggy of white powder out of her pussy and held it underneath the bar to show Cherry.

"What the hell is that?"

"It's called White Monkey. It's a blend of coke, meth, and Adderall. It gives you that extra boost of energy and keeps you woke."

"Aw, hell nah! Bitch, I ain't no dope head. I want to get my man's money, but I'm not finna be strung out like some crack whore to get it."

Sugar laughed, finding her innocence amusing. "Look at me, hon. Do I look like some junky or dope head whore to you? I use this shit all the time. How else do you think I have the energy to hustle like I do?"

Cherry thought about Sugar's expensive boob job, convertible Jaguar, and name brand lifestyle and couldn't imagine she used. She reminded Cherry nothing of the dope head whores she was used to seeing - the whores with missing teeth, bad skin, cheap pussy, and who sold all they owned for their next high. No, Sugar looked nothing like them.

"No. But I'm good. I'll just keep popping the No Doze and drinking Red Bulls and sleeping when I can."

"Next to the stage is the beautiful Ms. Cherry Bottom," the DJ announced.

"Well, that's me. I'll talk to you later." Cherry got out of her seat ready to make her way to the stage.

"Okay, babes." Sugar watched Cherry walk towards the stage as a young Mexican man with a long ponytail took a seat at the bar next to Sugar.

"You got the bitch fixed yet?" The man picked up Sugar's drink and gulped it down.

"Not yet, baby. But trust me, Los, the way she going, it won't be long before she'll be needing us to give her that extra boost to keep going. And then we'll have her hook, line, and sinker."

Los called the bartender over to refill his drink. Then Los told Sugar to pay him. Sugar rolled her eyes, then pulled some money out her bra and paid the bartender.

"Sugar, you know if we gonna make it big out here. We got to get all the bitches we can hooked on this shit. The more bitches we turn into junkies, the closer we get to the life we want."

Sugar rubbed her hands on his chest. "I know, baby. We still going to move to Beverly Hills and make me a movie star, right?"

Los took her arms and wrapped them around him. "Of course, mami. You know I'm going to make sure you become the next big thing in Hollywood. But we can't accomplish that unless you get these bitches hooked."

Sugar picked up his drink and watched Cherry perform as she sipped it. "Don't worry, baby, I got you."

***

Boss was awakened from his nap by the sounds of his phone ringing. He wiped the sleep from his eyes as he answered the phone.

"Talk to me."

"Did I wake you?"

Boss looked at the caller ID on the phone and didn't recognize the number. "Who is this?"

"You forgot the sound of my voice after all these years?"

Boss sat up in bed as it dawned on him who the caller was. "Queenie. What's good, baby?"

"I got the day off from work today and I was wondering if you wanted to hang out?"

"It depends."

"On what?"

"On whether or not we can pick up where we left off at in life."

"We can talk about all that when you get here."

Boss could feel her smile through the phone. He scribbled down her address and jumped in the shower.

The address Queenie gave him led to a ranch style house in the quiet suburban neighborhood of Wauwatosa. Cobblestones paved the walkway leading to the front door. An array of colorful flowers blossomed in a small garden in the front yard. A beautiful sound chimed when Boss rang the doorbell. Seconds later, Queenie appeared in the doorway dressed in a short black Versace dress that paid homage to every curve of her body. Her breasts looked as if they were going to pop out like a can of biscuits.

She welcomed Boss in. Inside, the smell of vanilla adorned the air.

"This a nice little pad. Whose is it?"

"It's all mines. My grandma owned a few properties and left me this one when she passed."

After a quick tour, Boss and Queenie played a game of catch up and reminisce. Having enough fill of the game, Boss decided it was time to wrap that mummy back into the bandages of his game.

"I grew a lot in the pimping game since then, baby. I'm headed to the top to become king pimp. And as they say, every king needs a queen. So let's be that team we were back then, but even greater."

"I don't know about all that, Boss. We were kids back then. Sins of a kid is innocent and can be forgiven. But I'm a grown woman now. A godly woman. And I've made a positive representation for myself since way back then."

Boss stood up and straightened his clothes. "Look here, Queenie baby, all this reminiscing has been a fun walk down memory lane. But the past is gone, and my eyes is on the future. And if you want to be a part of that future, then it's a must that you submit to this pimping of mines. My heart still flutters for you, baby. But I have no vacancies in my life for a square bitch."

He kissed her behind the ear before walking out of her life. He knew her feelings for him reigned as true for him as his for her, but he couldn't give in. The pimp in him refused to bow to square emotions. With her being a devout Christian, Boss knew to get her, he would have to battle God for control over the bitch.

***

The next night, Cherry sat in the dressing room in front of the vanity mirror with her head down. She was feeling completely drained already and the night hadn't even begun. A convention was in town that night, and that meant the club would be packed. And with the quota Boss gave her to make, she needed all the energy she could get.

Sugar entered the dressing room and saw Cherry looking all burnt out. "Hon, you okay?"

Cherry looked up at Sugar with pleading eyes. "You said that shit you got will wake me up?"

"Babes, this shit here will wake you and give you the energy and stamina of a god." Sugar pulled out a bag of White Monkey. She made up six lines of the powder. She snorted three of the lines, then passed the straw to Cherry. "You see? It's that easy."

Cherry stared down at the little white lines on the back of a CD case for a second before putting the straw to her first line. It wasn't as bad as she thought it would be. Cherry quickly snorted the last two lines just as the DJ called her to the stage. As soon as her hand gripped the pole and the music started to play, the White Monkey kicked in. She began to feel herself. As the music played, she went into a zone and lost herself in the moment. When the music stopped, she looked around and saw the whole club erupting in cheers, and money covered the stage. She knew then she found just what she needed to help her stay on top of her game.

Los sparked a cigarette as he leaned against the bar and watched Cherry's performance with Sugar. "It seems like we got a new customer."

"I told you, baby, that I got this. I knew it wouldn't be long before she'd come around."

Los took a pull of his cigarette. "Now that she's had a taste, I want you to start little by little easing heroin into her mix. That will give her that need to keep coming back."

"Will do." Sugar placed her empty glass on the counter and Los slapped her on her little pink ass as she walked off.

He couldn't believe how dumb and blind she was to his true intentions. Unknown to Sugar, Los was already married with three kids, and all he wanted was to make enough bread to bring his family over from Mexico to live a comfortable life. He figured if he could make a quarter of a million, that would be enough to ditch the li'l ditzy pink bitch, then open up a small business and start a new life with his family in another state. All he needed was to make another hundred grand and with good hustling hoes like Cherry and a few others, it wouldn't be long before he reached that goal. Los didn't have a pimp bone in his body, but the dope he was pushing was all the game he needed to break a bitch.

***

It'd been three weeks since Cherry first nosedived into the White Monkey and she hadn't been without it since. Lately she began to feel as if she couldn't go without it. Sugar, knowing that Cherry was hooked, introduced her to Los a couple weeks ago so she could start buying directly from him.

While giving a lap dance to a customer, she saw Los come into the club and she immediately started to feels antsy to blow a couple of lines. As soon as the song ended, she snatched the extra tip from the customer and hurried off. She ran up to one of the other dancers. "Lulu, you seen Los?"

"He's in the back getting Sugar together." She pointed to the dressing room.

Only dancers were allowed in the dressing room, but Los tipped the bouncers good to look the other way when he went back there and handled business. And most of the girls didn't mind because they were copping from Los too.

Walking into the dressing room, Cherry spotted Los blowing lines of coke off a small pocket mirror with Sugar sitting on his lap.

"Los, let me get a ball." Cherry stood there counting her money.

Los held up one finger, then dove into a line of coke. He lifted his head and squeezed the tip of his nose, then sniffed in each of his nostrils one by one . "Shoot me two Bens and I'll get you right."

"$200 for a ball?"

"Cherry, this is White Monkey, not coke. You want the good shit, you got to pay for it."

"Fine! Just make sure every gram is there."

They made the exchange, then Sugar and Los left the dressing room. Cherry pulled up a chair and began forming five thin lines of the powder. In the midst of blowing her last line, one of the new dancers walked in and stopped in her tracks at the site of Cherry blowing. Cherry looked up at her with powder still caked in her nostrils.

"Bitch, what you looking at?"

The new girl ignored her and walked on past to change her outfit.

"Yeah, bitch, keep going with yo' nosy ass." Cherry sniffed in the leftover residue in her nostrils.

Instantly feeling her high, she got up too fast and stumbled a little. The new girl chuckled and shook her head at the shame of it all. Feeling angered by her slight embarrassment, Cherry turned her rage to her.

"Oh, bitch, I'm funny to you?"

The new girl looked up at Cherry while she put on her thigh high boots. "Nah li'l mama. And by the way, you ain't got to refer to me as bitch. My name is Gorgeous."

Cherry stepped up to her and looked her over. "Gorgeous, huh? Well, you stay yo' pretty ass out my way and mind yo' business. I would hate to fuck a bitch up for getting between me and my money. You know what I mean?"

Gorgeous stood up in her six-inch heeled boots, towering over Cherry's 5'4" frame by nearly 8 inches.

"It's Cherry, right?"

Cherry folded her arms across her chest and looked Gorgeous up and down.

Taking that as a yes, Gorgeous continued. "What you do with yo' body is your business, and I could give a fuck less. But ain't no money in this bitch yours unless it's in yo' G-string. So you can keep yo' drug-induced threats to yourself! Because trust me, I'm not the bitch you want to fuck with."

Cherry was ready to vomit words of venom back at Gorgeous, but was stopped when the manager walked into the dressing room.

"Why the hell are you girls still back here? We have a full house tonight. So get your asses out there now!"

Cherry turned to the manager. "I'm coming now, Johnny."

"You better, because if the two of you aren't out here in the next two minutes, tip-out will be double." Johnny put his cigar in his mouth and left.

Cherry spun back around to face Gorgeous. "Just stay out my way." Cherry sized her up again, then left.

King Dream

CHAPTER 9

Though the game had been looking good for Boss lately, he knew that didn't mean to let his guard down. The Holy Bible Of Game taught him that a pimp must stay on his toes at all times and never trust a hoe. Because of that, he'd been doing all he could to stay ten steps ahead of his bitches. He'd been having Macita and Coco in St. Louis for almost a week now and for two days, he'd been keeping an eye on them without them knowing. Last night he watched as they left the club and turned tricks throughout the night at their hotel room. By all accounts, the hoes were doing what they were supposed to be doing. But a hoe could always do better.

Boss and Polo pulled up to Club Roxy's. "I know we ain't finna do another stalker's night on these hoes. I'm tired of sitting in this damn car."

"Nah, tonight we going in the club. I want to see how these hoes be performing inside the clubs when I'm not around. It's Friday and it's going to be packed in all these clubs around here tonight, so we'll be able to blend in with the crowd."

"Oh hell yeah! Now that's what I'm talking about. A nigga gets to see some bitches!"

The song "Sex Metal Barbie" by the band In This Moment blasted through the speakers as they walked into the club. A Gothic-looking white girl with short black hair, big gauge ear piercings, and tattoo danced on the main stage. The girl had a body that only a Catholic priest could love. She was flat-chested with no ass, but a large crowd was formed around this bitch, who had a body of a twelve-year-old boy.

Just as Boss thought, the club was packed, but he was able to spot Macita with no problem. She was tending to a customer seated at a table towards the middle of the club. Boss and Polo stayed ducked off in the shadows of the club. Boss watched Macita until she got off stage and started making her rounds around the club, collecting tips for her performance. He and Polo slipped out of the club and went down the street to the Pink Slip.

In St. Louis, there were three strip clubs on one particular block. You had PT's, Roxy's, and the Pink Slip. To classify these clubs in terms of music categories, PT's would be the pop, Taylor Swift club type, Roxy's would be the rock & roll, Marilyn Manson type, and the Pink Slip would be the hip hop, Li'l Jon type club. When they entered the Pink Slip, Coco was entertaining a customer with a lap dance. Just as they did at Roxy's, Boss and Polo posted up in the shadows. Unlike Roxy's, the women in the Pink Slip were thick as Snickers bars.

"Yo, I'm going to catch up with you in a minute. I see something I like."

"Just try not to let Coco see you. I ain't done checking her hustle."

"Aye-aye, captain." Polo gave him a two-finger salute before walking off to the other end of the club.

Boss watched Coco just like he did with Macita. He was seeing how they got down and taking mental notes of the things he wanted them to improve on. He watched as niggas in the club grabbed on Coco, trying to catch free feels and try to get a free or cheap fuck out of her. Coco was handling herself well and doing everything he taught her to do in situations like those. He purposely sent her to that ghetto-ass club because she was fresh to the game and he wanted to thicken her skin. He figured if she could survive in the jungle, then she would do well just about anywhere.

Ten minutes later, Polo returned to the table with the smile of a virgin who just got laid.

"What put the cheese on yo' cracker, player?"

"I just bagged that redbone right over there." Polo pointed to a thick redbone with red hair.

"Yeah, she something nice. Thick as a bitch too. What she talking about?"

"I told her I'm a pimp and ran a little spiel to her and she bit game. She said she wants to kick it with me when she gets off and see what's up."

A petite caramel skin dancer with a Betty Boop hairstyle and tattoo on her neck approached them. "Y'all want a lap dance?" She turned around and made her ass clap for them.

Boss looked the other way, ignoring her.

"We good, baby." Polo gave her a dollar and she moved on to the next potential customer.

Boss returned to their conversation. "So you a pimp now, Polo?"

"The way I see it, if you can do it and make good with it, what's keeping me from achieving the same success?"

Boss took notice weeks ago that Polo had been taking interest in the pimp game, but Boss never thought he would try to act on it. "I know this shit looks fun and exciting, but Polo, this game is serious, man. It ain't for everybody. This ain't no suit you can just put on. This shit got to be in you, not on you." Polo gave Boss a sideways look.

"So what you saying is you don't think I got what it takes for this game?"

Everything in Boss wanted to say yes, but how could he kill the dreams of the man he looked at as his brother? He wanted to share his dream with him.

"Nah, brah, I wouldn't say all that. I just want you to be aware that this game ain't easy as it looks and hoes will always put you to the test. The hater cam is always on a playa. If you feel you can handle all the twisted mind games and other shit that comes with the game, then by all means, pimp on, baby."

Polo cracked a smile and shook hands with Boss. "Now that's what I wanted to hear."

"Good. Now let's get out this club before that hoe spots me."

They slipped out the door and make their way to the hotel.

***

They got to the hotel and Boss laid back in bed, blowing on a blunt of loud as he read the Holy Bible Of Game. Polo took up a room a few doors down with the li'l freak he knocked at the club.

A knock at the door took Boss out of his zone. He knew it couldn't be nobody else but Polo.

"Who I look like, Mr. Belvedere? Nigga, use yo' key!" Boss yelled towards the door, then put his head back in the book. A brief pause, then the knocking started again. "Damn it, Polo, I swear——" Boss started to say as he swung the door open, but then was immediately taken aback by who he saw standing in front of him.

"Knock, knock. Sorry, it's not Polo. Now are you going to continue to stand there with that look of shock on your face, or are you going to invite me in?"

"Queenie, what are you doing here? Better yet, how the hell you know where to find me?"

Queenie pushed past Boss and plopped down on the bed. "I have my sources."

"My mama told you where to find me, huh?"

"Maybe." She shrugged her shoulders.

Boss closed the door and walked over to where she sat. "Okay, you found me, so now what?"

She picked his blunt up out the ashtray and fired it back to life. She hit the blunt, then blew out a cloud of smoke.

"Saint Queenie taking up the herb? Now what will the congregation at that church you attend think of that?"

"I haven't been too honest with you, Boss. There's no church." She uncrossed her legs and stood up. She walked past Boss, brushing against him with the affection of a cat begging to be scratch by its master. She took the bottle of Remy off the table and poured them both a drink. "I'm not a Christian. That was all bullshit I was feeding you."

Boss stood confused. She passed him a drink. "I don't understand. Why lie about something like that?"

"Boss, when I left Milwaukee, I never stopped loving you. I thought about you and all the plans we had together. I never stopped believing in you. I never stopped wanting to be that woman who helped push you to the top of the game. Over these past years, me and your mama stayed in touch. She used to tell me how she seen herself in me and saw the love her and your father had for each other in us. So over the years, she's been grooming me to be the baddest bitch in the game and to take you to the top. The whole lie about me being an innocent Christian girl was all your mama's idea. She didn't want it to be easy for you. She wanted to see when you are given the choice between your heart and the game, what would you choose."

"And?"

"And just liked she hoped, you chose the game like a true pimp would. She said your father would've been proud. I know I am."

With the grace of a panther creeping up on its prey, she approached Boss and put her lips to his. The sweet taste of her lips on his gave him instant wood. He held her in his arms as his hands explored the curves of her body.

"Hold up, baby. If you are going to be my woman, then we going to start this shit off the right way. Bitch, pop that purse open and choose up!"

"That's just what a hoe been waiting to hear you say." She opens up her purse and withdrew five bundles of cash and handed it to Boss. The bands wrapped around the money let him know it was a total of fifty grand she was giving him. "Some of it is hoe money and the rest came from what my grandmother left me."

Boss held his feelings of surprise inside. This was the most bread a hoe ever gave him. "Bitch, it came from a hoe, so it's all hoe money to me," Boss said nonchalantly as he put the money in the hotel room safe.

He then turned to Queenie and caressed her lips with his. She melted right in his arms. His hands found the zipper on the back of her purple and gold Prada dress. She pulled her arms out of the sleeves and the dress fell to the floor. He scooped her up and laid her on the bed. His tongue knew no bounds as it laid wet trails all over her body. Her eyes rolled in the back of her head and she let out a loud moan as her womb made room for him. He gave her long, deep strokes and her juices began to splash all over him. He forgot how good it felt to be inside her. Her sexy moans increased his need for her. He spun her over and hit her from the back. His strokes became harder and faster and she threw her ass back at him as they both gave chase to their orgasms. Moments later, the chase ended as they both erupted into long moans like two wolves howling at a full moon. Then they clasped onto the bed and marinated in the passion of their ecstasy throughout the night.

CHAPTER 10

Boss awakened the next morning with Queenie asleep on his chest. He checked the time: 9:26 a.m. Macita and Coco should've made it back to the city hours ago and he couldn't wait to tally up the bread they made. He woke Queenie up with a slap on the ass. "Rise and grind, baby."

She looked up at Boss, squinting to adjust her sleeping eyes to the light. She yawned and stretched her arms. "What time is it?"

"Time to rule the world, baby. Now get that ass up and let's get this money."

She smiled and kissed his chest. "Okay, daddy."

They hopped in the shower, got dressed, then parted ways. He went down the way and knocked on Polo's room door. He answered the door still half asleep.

"What up? It ain't checkout time, is it?"

"For a pimp chasing a bread truck it is. Come on. We got to get back to the city. I got some bread to get."

"Just give me like fifteen minutes."

A soft whimper came from the bed. Boss looked past Polo and saw the redbone laid out naked in the bed, tangled in the sheets asleep. "Better make that thirty minutes." Polo grinned.

Boss frowned and walked off.

Forty minutes passed by and Polo still hadn't come out. Boss was getting close to kicking in the door and dragging his ass out of there, but seconds later, out came Polo and the redbone. He escorted her to a white Tahoe truck. He hugged and kissed her goodbye before jumping in the car with Boss.

"Man, shorty can't get enough of yo' boy!"

"Look, bruh, next time you want to wet yo' dick, do that shit on your own time and dime. You get me!" The agitation in Boss's voice killed Polo's excitement.

"Damn, pimp, what's all the hostility about?"

"I told you I had money to go get. A pimp never trusts a bitch with his bread for longer than he has to. Money is options, and those options gives a hoe too much temptation."

"You right, bruh, my bad. You know I'm still learning the game."

And that's what really bothered Boss. In this game, mistakes could rarely be afforded. The wrong decision could have you sitting behind bars for biblical years or get you killed. Boss feared such punishments the pimp gods could rain down on Polo for breaking the commandments of the game.

"We cool?" Polo held out his hand.

"Yeah, we cool." Boss slapped his hand. "Tell me what happened last night with you and that freak?"

"Princess? Oh! My nigga, we get to the room, right? And I keep running my little spiel on her about how I'm a pimp and need the right hoe in my life. She gave me this whole story about how she been in the game five years and been with a few pimps before who promised to spoil her and treat her right, but ended up fucking her over. And says she's really feeling me, but she's scared of getting fucked over again. I ran a little more game on her about how I'm not like them and with me, I'll give her all the love and care she needs. Then before she could say another word, I kissed her, and the next thing you know, we fucking like two dogs in heat. I mean, I'm tearing that ass up. I had that hoe calling me daddy and saying she chooses me. Then this morning, I fucked her again, and this time she broke bread and gave me all the money she had. Look here: $680." Polo flashed the bread he got out of Princess.

"Polo, would you let yo' bitch fuck a trick before she gets paid?"

"Hell nah! Even a rookie like me knows not to do that."

"Why not?"

"He could dip off on the hoe without paying her."

"Then why would you fuck a hoe who ain't paid you? You got to lead by example, my nigga. First impressions are everything. How you start off with a bitch is how you'll finish with her. And never tell a hoe you need her. Because a hoe could make bread, but she could never make a pimp. And just because a hoe calls you daddy don't mean you a pimp." Boss wanted to tell him that Princess had more money than she gave him. He could tell by the whole night's scenario that Polo just laid out that she was running her own little harmless game on him. Boss figured some things, a man must figure out for himself.

"That makes sense to me. I can really dig this pimping shit, man. I mean, look at all the perks to it. You get to have all these women, they bring you money, give you good bed and head, you travel all over, the fame and love. Man, this where it's at."

"Any real pimp will tell you it's only one perk to this game, and that's the money. And when you start thinking like that, you will start having things like this." Boss passed Polo a small travel bag. He looked inside and his eyes went wide.

"Damn, what's this, about 30 G's?"

"Try 50. Queenie popped up last night with it and chose up."

"Get the fuck out of here! She just gave you all this?"

"Believe that. You see, when a thoroughbred hoe knows she got a real stomp down pimp, she plays no games and gives all she has to make his visions a reality."

"Damn, my nigga. You really on yo' way to the top."

"I spent enough time at the bottom. It's time to claim my real spot in life with no looking back."

And that's just what Boss was going to do.

***

Cherry stepped out of the dressing room after nose vacuuming six lines of White Monkey. Her tolerance was quickly increasing. Before, three or four lines would've had her good for the night. Now that was just an appetizer. She was running through a sixteenth a night.

She was making her rounds through the club when she saw Gorgeous with one of her exclusive customers. "That punk bitch!" Cherry rushed her way across the club towards Gorgeous. She pushed Gorgeous, almost knocking her off balance.

"Bitch, I told you to stay out my way!"

Gorgeous gained her balance and sent a hard slap across Cherry's face. Cherry grabbed her and they wrestled to the floor. The audience threw money and cheered them on. The bouncer started to break it up, but seeing the excitement in the club and all the money being thrown around, the manager stalled the bouncer for a few moments.

Boss came out of the bathroom to the sounds of bottles breaking, screams, and loud cheers. He saw a crowd formed on the other side of the club and went to see what all the excitement was about. When he saw Cherry on the ground, he pushed his way through the crowd and pulled *Queenie* aka Gorgeous off of Cherry.

"What the fuck is going on?"

Cherry got back to her feet and straightened her hair. "This bitch trying to eat off my plate." Cherry pointed at her exclusive customer.

"Bitch, I already told you, unless it's in your G-string, it ain't yours! Ain't no boundaries on my daddy's pimping and it damn sho' ain't none on my hoeing. So I'm going to get all the money I can get." Gorgeous turned to Boss. "Ain't that right, daddy?"

"DADDY? Hoe, that's my daddy. I'm Boss's bottom bitch!"

"Boss, this the hoe you wanted me to meet?" Gorgeous looked confused.

"Yeah. Cherry, this is Queenie. Queenie, that's Cherry. Queenie is a part of this family. Now whatever beef you hoes got ends here and now. Do I make my mothafuckin' self clear?" Boss eyed both of them until he got his answer.

They both said "yes daddy" in unison.

Boss took off, leaving Queenie and Cherry to settle their differences.

"You don't like me, and I damn sho' could give a fuck less about you. But we seem to be stuck together. So I'm gonna make this real clear, bitch. You put yo' dope habit to rest today. I'm not going to let anything keep my man from getting to the top, especially no junkie-ass whore."

"I'm no junkie, bitch. I'm his bottom bitch. So recognize which one of us hoes run this shit. And what are you going to do anyway if I don't? Tell Boss on me?"

"Try me and see." Queenie pushed past her, ending the conversation.

Blood and Games

***

It had been a month since Polo bagged Princess and he came to find the game ain't as easy as he thought it would be. At the barbershop, he expressed his frustrations to Boss as he gave him a shave.

"What's good, P? You look a bit stressed. I don't see that usual smile on your face?"

"That bitch Princess ain't producing like I thought she would."

"What, you thought that one bitch was going to make you rich?"

"Let's say I didn't think I would lose money by having the bitch. I find myself having to come out of pocket for shit. Hell, sometimes this bitch don't make enough to cover tip-out at the club."

"Damn, sounds like you got a lazy hoe. What you going to do about it, pimp?"

"You tell me. Why you think I'm telling yo' ass about my troubles in the first place? It ain't to be social, mothafucka. Help a nigga out."

"Look, bruh, I can't pimp for the both of us. You got to put yo' own game to work." Boss didn't want to ignore Polo's call for help, but all his mind could reflect on was how his father's biggest mistake was giving his game to Rome. And the outcome of that wasn't the same fate he wanted for him and Polo.

"So you going to just let me keep taking losses with her when you know what I can do to wake and break this bitch?" Polo finished lining Boss's goatee.

"If I tell you what I would do to get the hoe right, then it ain't you pimping the bitch. It's me." Boss checked his fresh in the mirror.

"That hoe won't know."

Boss turned to Polo. "I hope you don't truly believe that. A hoe's eyes are always open, even when she's asleep. A bitch notices everything and is always looking for flaws in a pimp." He paid Polo and exited the barbershop with Polo following behind.

"Then just tell me what you'd do and I'll put my own spin on it. Come on, Boss, I need you on this one, bruh. Don't let me down. You know we go way back like afros and stacks."

Boss debated in his head whether or not to go against his first thoughts and take a chance on giving Polo the game he needed. He did what he thought best. "Get in the car, nigga, so I can put yo' square ass on game.

Polo's smile returned to his face for the first time that day.

Rome was always a snake deep down. And me and Polo are way too tight to ever fall apart like that, Boss thought to himself, and he prayed it was true.

***

Polo came home to find Princess still in bed asleep. She only made $80 the night before and half of that had to go on gas. He had about enough of her shit. SMACK! He slapped her on her bare ass as hard as he could.

"Bitch, get yo' lazy ass up!"

She sat up in bed as quickly as she could and tried to rub away the sting on her ass. "Aw, Polo, what the fuck!"

"Bitch, it's 5:37 in the evening and yo' punk ass ain't accomplished shit but a dream!"

"Baby, you know I had a long night last night and I'm tired."

"Yeah, you tired, alright, and I'm tired of you. Either you shape up and get with my program, or you take yo' funky ass back to St. Louis and find yourself a chump who wants a worthless-ass hoe like you."

"Nigga, if I leave, my truck is coming with me and you can go back to catching rides with Boss!"

Polo got in her face. "Bitch, that makes me no mind. It'll still be better than putting up with a bitch who wants nothing more out of life than a wet ass and chump change. So take yo' raggedy-ass truck, bitch. I can get further in life without you or it."

Sensing the seriousness in Polo's voice and demeanor, she tried seduction to ease the situation into her favor.

"Damn, bae, stop being so grumpy." She wrapped her arms around him. "I know what's wrong. My baby needs some cookie.

Come here so I can put a smile on your face. I'll do that li'l thing you like I do with my cookie muscles."

Polo pushed her away. "Pussy don't move me. You want to impress me, show me the value in cash that pussy possesses. I'd had enough of that coochie, but I could never have enough money. Now get yo' ass up and show me you're more than a $80 a night hoe or hit the bricks, bitch!"

Polo then walked away, leaving Princess shocked.

***

Later that night, Polo picked Princess up from the club. He hadn't said a word to her since he checked her earlier. She saw then that Polo was serious about leaving her if she didn't fall in line and get her hustle up.

"Hey daddy! How was your night?" Polo ignored her. "Polo! Talk to me, bae. Look, I got on my hustle tonight. I made $670." She handed him the money. "At least smile to let me know you're proud of me."

"Smile? Bitch, for what? You had one decent night. Now what, you go back to being a lazy bitch? If that's the case, you can keep this shit and take it back to St. Louis with you."

Her heart was pained when he threw the money back at her. She knew then all games had to come to an end and he was serious about his pimping. He had been good to her - in fact, better than the pimps she fucked with in the past. She didn't want to lose him. With tears in her eyes, she picked up the money and put it back into his hand. She grabbed his face, trying to get him to look at her.

"Daddy, no, I'm gonna hustle my ass off from now on. I just got too comfortable with your loving, baby. I'm sorry if I took advantage of you in any way. Just don't give up on us before giving me a chance to make things right. Please, daddy?"

Polo was glad Boss changed his mind about telling him exactly what to do. His lines worked like a shaman's charm on her. What he found crazy was that Boss knew exactly what the hoe would do and say.

"Fair enough. I'll give you one more and ONLY one more chance. Don't make me regret this, Princess."

She wrapped her arms around him as tight as she could and kissed him. "I won't, daddy, I promise."

CHAPTER 11

After clearing 15 Gs for the week, Boss decided to take the girls for a night out. They hit up Club Rave with Polo and Princess. He wanted his team looking their best, so they went to Mall Of America to do some shopping.

As they browsed through the Gucci store, Princess approached Coco. "Hey girl!"

"Hey!"

"That's a cute top. It'll look good on you too."

Coco was admiring a red and gold Gucci tube top. "It would, wouldn't it?"

"No doubt." Princess was trying to butter her up so she could hit her with her real intentions for their conversation. "So how long you been with Boss?"

"It's been a few months now."

"That's what's up. You seem happy."

"I am more than happy. Boss has been good to me. I do what I'm supposed to do and get his money and he makes sure I don't need or want for shit. The man spoils me."

They moved down to check out another rack of clothes.

"I feel you girl. Me and Polo haven't got to that level yet where we can afford to be so spoiled."

"Don't trip. The two of you will get there. Polo's good peoples and you got a lot of hustle in you. You'll eventually know the feeling."

"Oh, don't get me wrong, I've been with pimps before that had spoiled me. But it was because they were, let me say, lacking in other departments." They both laughed.

"I'm glad I don't have to worry about that at all." She leaned over and whispered to Princess. "Bitch, Boss is hung like an African horse and works it like a slave under a whip."

"Well damn, you are spoiled." That's exactly what Princess wanted to hear. Lately, she'd been growing a longing for Boss. She'd been checking him out and feeling his swag. She'd been curious if he was just as good of a lover as he was a pimp. Coco gave her the confirmation she needed, and now her craving for him had gone into overdrive. She watched as him and Polo conversed a few sections over. She gazed down at the bulge in his pants and the juices between her legs began to flow.

"Princess!" Coco yelled, snapping Princess out of a daze.

"Huh?"

"Damn, girl, you so busy looking at Polo you didn't hear me talking to you?"

"My bad, girl. That man be having me going sometimes. What were you saying?"

***

Meanwhile, Cherry had been trying to kick her habit for over a week and she was starting to feel why they called the shit White Monkey. She couldn't seem to shake it loose. Before they left for the mall, she called Sugar up and had her bring her a fifty piece to knock the edge off. She didn't have enough time to do it before they left, so she snuck off to the bathroom for a quick hit of the booger sugar.

Queenie saw her leave and had a feeling she was up to no good. She'd been noticing her eagerness to get away since they got there, so she followed her to the bathroom.

Queenie entered the bathroom. The restroom seemed to be quiet and empty except for a snorting noise echoing from the last stall. Queenie shook the stall door, but it was locked.

"This spot's occupied."

Queenie shook the door again.

"Are you fucking deaf? I said it's occupied, go away!" Cherry then heard heels on the tile floor walking away. "Dumb bitch." She went back to her lines, but before she could finish her second line, the stall door had burst open, making her jump and her powdery lines fall to the floor. She saw that it was Queenie. "You bitch! Look what you made me do!" Cherry dove to the floor, trying to find enough powder to scrape back into lines. As she put her nose and straw to the floor, she noticed Queenie taking video footage with her phone. "What the fuck do you think you're doing?"

"Getting all the evidence I need to show Boss the anchor around his ankle."

"You punk bitch!" Cherry charged at her, but Queenie side-stepped just in time, making Cherry crash into the sink. Queenie snatched her by the neck and slammed her against the wall.

"The way I see it, you got two choices. You either tell Boss you want to step down as bottom bitch and still be a part of this family. Or I text this video to him and...well, you know what will happen to you if he finds out you been getting high and cuffing money from him to do so. Tick, tick, tick." Queenie shook her head and finger at Cherry.

"Bitch, how dare you try to blackmail me?"

"Yeah, I know, it's a bitch, ain't it. So what's it gonna be, Cherry? I text him or you step down?"

Cherry yanked Queenie's hand off her neck. "Fine! You win! I'll step down!"

"Good. Have it done before we get to the club tonight. Oh, and your days of getting high are over with, or you are off this team for good. Now don't forget to wash your hands before leaving out." Queenie straightening her clothes, then exited the restroom.

Cherry hurled her makeup mirror at the door in frustration as the door closed behind Queenie. She was pissed that Queenie had beaten her out of her position.

Cherry straightened herself up and left the restroom. She spotted the group making their way towards the escalator. She caught up to Boss and tapped him on the shoulder. "I gotta holla at you about something important."

"We headed to the food court. When we get our food, you and I will sit down and rap about whatever's on your mind."

They get to the food court and grabbed something to eat from Panda Express. Boss and Cherry sat alone at a table away from the rest of the girls. Boss took a bite of his sweet and sour chicken and washed it down with a swallow of Sprite. "What is it you want to talk about?"

Cherry stirred her rice around her plate with her fork as she spoke. "I can't do this anymore."

"You can't do what?"

"I can't be your bottom bitch anymore. I can't handle it, it's too much responsibility for me. I'm tired all the time and barely have the energy to make my quarter. I think it's best that I step down. I like it better just being a regular whore." She couldn't even look him in the face when she told him. She felt if she did, she would fall apart.

"You sure about this?"

She nodded her head.

"Alright, then as of now, Queenie's bottom bitch. I'll let her and other girls know when we leave."

Cherry raised her head and looked in Queenie's direction. Queenie was looking right at her with smiling eyes. Cherry wondered if she was to rip that pretty face of hers off, would Boss still love that hoe then?

They hit the club later that night. Boss got two VIP tables: one for him and Polo and one for the girls. He instantly became the target of all eyes as he entered the club dressed in all white Gucci with a red mink coat and matching red Gucci belt and shoes. His iced-out gold presidential Rolex shined like a disco ball. An iced-out chain with a charm of a king on a throne with each of his feet resting on a bitch and reading Boss Bandz hung low on his chest. Both his pinkies glistened with diamonds. One of the rings, a crown encrusted in diamonds, belonged to his father, Big Bandz. All four of his women wore the same colors as him.

Isis and Peaches were perched in one section of VIP entertaining their next Charlie vics when Peaches spotted Boss and Polo walk into the club with some girls. She leaned over and whispered in Isis's ear. "Ain't that Boss and Polo?"

Isis craned her neck around the club. "Where?"

"Over there on the other side of VIP."

Isis's eyes followed the nod of Peaches's head and she found them. "I see them."

"It looks like he stepped his game up," Peaches added in.

"Yeah, but he's still a nobody. Don't nobody in this game recognize his ass. And besides, he ain't got shit on Rome." Isis acted like she wasn't impressed with Boss, but found herself unable to take her eyes off him. There was something different about him that she couldn't quite put a finger on. He had a more powerful essence than he did the last time she had seen him.

Polo leaned over and said something to Boss. Then Boss's eyes caught hers and suddenly, she felt small and worthless to his presence. She finally broke her trance and looked away. She took a swallow of her drink, then took a quick look back at Boss. She saw him saying something in the ear of a sexy mixed breed chick that had walked in with him. Isis then gave her attention back to her guest.

A few minutes later, five girls approached their table. The sexy mixed breed Boss had whispered to moments ago spoke.

"Excuse me, gentlemen, I was wondering, why are the two of you chilling with only two women when you could have more fun with the five of us?"

The taller man of the two then spoke. "Well baby, these women are treating us tonight."

"Really? Well, I'm sure two bright players like yourselves made sure of that by checking with the VIP hostess. I mean, I would hate for you players to get Charlied with what looks to be a very expensive night. You see our table over there is covered with a three thousand dollar prepaid tab." Queenie attempted to hand him the receipt, but Isis snatched it from her and got in her face.

"And just what the fuck you think you doing?"

"I'm going to be putting a hoe like you in her proper place if you don't step back. You ran that Charlie game on my man, so I'm hitting yo' ass with the reverse Charlie."

"You weak-ass bitch! You think I can't afford this shit? I'm Isis, damn it! I'm the baddest bitch in the game."

"You used to be. But now Queen Bandz is here. Recognize when yo' time is up, you washed-up bitch." Queenie turned her back on Isis and walked off with the other girls in tow.

The two men got up and followed behind the train of the five women.

Isis frowned. "And where the hell y'all think y'all going?"

The shorter one answered. "We players, baby. You ain't finna kill our rep with a Charlie." Then he turned and followed the others.

Isis looked across the room at Boss, who was standing there sipping his drink and watching everything unfold. He flashed her a devious smile and winked at her. The hostess came over and handed Isis a $3600 bill. Isis snatched the bill from her. She paid the bill and stormed out of the club with Peaches.

As Boss's women, along with Princess, entertained and ravaged the pockets of the fake pimps they had lifted from Isis and Peaches, Queenie walked over to his table. "Daddy, can we spit for a minute?"

Boss motioned his hand for her to come take a seat next to him. "You come to explain to me how you got my bottom bitch to step down?"

"And what would make you think that I had something to do with me?"

"Because I know you. You will always do whatever it takes to make yourself number one in my life. And that hoe there hates to feel like any woman in my life is above her. So for her to tell me she wants to step down from being bottom bitch tells me you must have some major dirt on that bitch."

"You want me to tell you what it is?"

"No, I don't give a fuck. That's hoe business. She fucked up somehow and you did what you had to do to secure your position. Making boss moves like that shows me you deserve to be in that position more than anyone." Boss took a sip of Remy and put his arm around Queenie. "Well, Gorgeous——" Boss started to say, but Queenie cut him off.

"Uh-uh, daddy. It's not Gorgeous no more. It's Queen Bandz now."

Boss couldn't hold back his smile due to how true that title rang for her. She managed to come into his fold and mentally defeat all his hoes to be his number one. She had indeed earned the title of Queen Bandz in his eyes.

"I like that. Every King needs a Queen. To Queen Bandz!" Boss got to his feet and raised a toast.

All the women and their guests at their table stood and joined the toast. Cherry sat quietly with a mug on her face, giving Queenie the evil eye.

"Thank you, daddy. But what I wanted to spit with you about is some business ideas I wanted to run by you."

"Tell me what's on yo' mind?"

Queenie spent most of the night whispering in his ear and breaking down her ideas to him. The other women enjoyed the night, but Cherry's blood boiled at how close Queenie was with Boss the whole night. She couldn't help but feel the pain of her demotion. She wasn't going to sit back and let Queenie destroy everything she worked hard for. She wasn't going to let her take Boss from her. She began to make plans in her mind to get rid of Queenie. One way or another, the bitch had to go.

King Dream

CHAPTER 12

Boss laid in bed studying The Holy Bible Of Game. His conversation with Queenie the night before at the club about taking the game to a new level, opened his mind to new vistas. He wanted to consult the Holy Bible Of Game for further wisdom. He was deep off into his studies when his phone rang.

"Hello?"

"Daddy, it's Coco."

"I got caller ID. I know who it is, bitch. Tell me something I don't know, like what the hell it is you want?"

"We have a problem down here at the club. Some pimp nigga here sweating Macita's heels hard."

"So what, bitch? That's what any nigga who calls himself pimping is supposed to do. Just make sure that hoe keeps her head down and stay on my money."

"That's the problem, Boss. The nigga's bread blocking her from getting money. Every trick that tries to spend money with her, he scares off. I tried to tell the bouncers, but they won't do shit about it."

That let Boss know the pimp on Macita's heels must've had the bouncers in his pockets. "Calm down! I'll be there in a minute. In the meantime, production don't stop. Keep my money coming." Boss hung up the phone and made his way to the club.

As soon as he stepped into the club, he was immediately approached by Coco as if she'd been hawking the door awaiting his arrival. "Boss, she's over there on the other side of the bar. You see that nigga in the Kangol hat and blue and white suit behind her? That's the pimp that's been on her ass. The other girls here told me he's a well-known pimp. They say his name is Break-A-Hoe."

Boss made strides over to where Macita and Break-A-Hoe were at. Unnoticed, he stood to the side and observed as Break-A-Hoe went in on Macita.

"Yeah, bitch, you gon' choose this pimp tonight. I'm going to keep rolling hard on your heels like rollerblades, hoe. Ain't no escaping this pimping."

Macita sat at the bar with her back to Break-A-Hoe ignoring him with the hopes that he would get tired of her rejection and leave her alone. But that didn't deter him. Break-A-Hoe grabbed her by the shoulder and snatched her around to face him. Macita jumped up.

"Pussy hunting-ass nigga, keep yo' damn hands off me. Or pay me like the rest of these niggas!"

"Bitch, who the fuck you talking to like that!"

Break-A-Hoe was a split second away from slapping her when Boss stepped in between them. Relief ran across Macita's face when she saw Boss. Boss removed his Versace frames from his face before speaking.

"Check this out, P. I got major respect for this here game. And as a pimp myself, I understand it's every P's duty to mack every bitch he sees fit. So mack at will, pimp. But this hoe here is mines. And she ain't trying to give you a date or time. Now I don't necessarily give a fuck about this bitch. But when you come between her and my money, you step yo' foot in some shit you don't really want to fuck with."

Break-A-Hoe took a step back and sized Boss up. "Nigga, I'm pimping Break-A-Hoe, the coldest gorilla pimp the game has ever named. And I know everybody in this game from Spain to Maine. Now ain't that strange that who you be is a mystery to me?"

"I'm Boss Bandz." Boss held his hand out.

Break-A-Hoe ignored his gentlemanly gesture and turned his head up arrogantly to the right and picked at his nails. "I've never heard of such a nigga."

Boss put his hand away and stepped forward, closing the gap in between them. "Now that you have, I expect that you will respect my hand in this game. Just as you would with your other fellow P's."

Break-A-Hoe's face balled up in disgust. "Respect yo' hand? Nigga, Break-A-Hoe is a real pimp. I don't respect no unknown nigga that claims he's pimping. If you want my respect, you got to prove your game to me."

"That ain't no issue for me. My game ain't mushy. In fact, it's tighter than virgin pussy. I guarantee you I can knock two of your bitches before you could ever knock one of mines."

Break-A-Hoe laughed at him. "Nigga, please, you ain't knocked a real pimp a day in your life. You fresh meat, mothafucka. Them Gators of yours probably never even bit into a hoe's ass before."

"Tell me something, P, does the name Pimping Memphis ring a bell for you?"

"Yeah, Pimping Memphis is a well-known player in the game. Now why would a John Doe like yourself want to know if I know him?"

Boss pointed to Macita. "Well, that pretty li'l bitch of mines that you been hounding all night…who you think I knocked her from?"

"You trying to tell me yo' fresh mouth ass knocked Memphis for this bitch? I have to call him to confirm such a thing, because lies like that can't be told."

"Do as you see fit, pimp." Boss adjusted the sleeves of his black Ferragamo suit jacket.

Break-A-Hoe pulled out his phone and dialed up Pimping Memphis. "Memph, how you do, baby? Yeah, this Break-A-Hoe. Listen, baby, I'm calling you because I have some fresh to the game stud here who calls himself Boss Bandz claiming he knocked you for a bitch. Yeah…yeah, well dig that. I been trying to put the bitch on hook all night. Alright, pimp, be easy. I'ma holla at you." Break-A-Hoe ended the call. "Well, it seems your tongue holds no lies. Memphis admits that you indeed knocked him for the bitch."

"Like I told you, my game is tight."

"I won't say all that. Yeah, you knocked Memphis, but that nigga's game ain't nothing spectacular. You want my respect, you got to knock an extraordinary stud whose game is hoe tested and pimp approved. Someone such as myself."

"Present me with the opportunity, and I'll show you my game is exceptional enough to knock any pimp's bitch."

"Ha ha! Boy, I like yo' confidence. Tell you what, baby, meet me here at closing time with all yo' hoes and I'll bring all mines. And we will have ourselves a little challenge. And may the best game win."

"I'll be here."

"Good, because I'ma call up some of my pimp buddies to come check out the show. So you better bring yo' A-game and try not to choke up, playa." Break-A-Hoe turned towards Macita. "You get ready to make your new home with me tonight, baby." He winked at her and smoothly strolled off.

Macita rolled her eyes at Break-A-Hoe then smiled and wrapped her arms around Boss. "Thank you, daddy! That mothafucka been hounding me all night. I'm so glad you came when you––"

Boss pushed her off him and grabbed her by the neck before she could finish her sentence. "Bitch, the next time a mothafucka comes between you and my money, you better gut they ass from the rooter to the tooter. Or the next time, you will find yo' funky ass on a slab at the morgue. You got me, bitch?"

Macita tried to nod her head yes. Boss pushed her away as he let go of her neck. "Now take yo' ass back out there and get my mothafuckin' money, bitch!"

Macita scurried off.

Boss was acting off a passage in the Holy Bible Of Game. Never let a hoe feel there's an excuse good enough for not having your money, and she will never give you one.

CHAPTER 13

Isis slid down the pole and danced to the song "WAP" by Cardi B. After she finished her set, she picked her money up off the floor. The DJ announced the next girl to the stage just as Isis stepped off.

A familiar face passed by her. They made eye contact and the woman gave Isis a con artist smile before taking to the stage.

Nechie's song "Nasty Wit' It" boomed through the club's speakers. The woman climbed the pole and slid down upside down, then cartwheeled into the splits, bouncing her ass, making the crowd erupt into cheers. She crawled over to a nerdy-looking white man with thick bifocals. She cruised her hand through his short-cropped hair and down his face, then cuffed his chin in her hands. "Tip me."

"Tip her, Tim!" His coworkers cheered him on.

Tim dug into his pockets and pulled out a dollar bill and gave it to her. She took it, ripped it up, and threw it back in his face. Then she took his hand and rubbed it slowly across her breasts as she moved her body to the music.

"I said tip me."

"Come on, Tim, you can do better than that. Be a man and pay for what you want, buddy." Tim's buddies cheered him on again.

Tim pulled out a ten dollar bill and handed it to her. She snatched it from him and shoved it in his mouth. "Can you eat that?"

Tim shook his head no.

She slapped him, then licked the side of his face. "Then don't feed that bullshit to me. Now tip me, damn it."

Tim wide-eyed and excitedly and nervously pulled out a twenty and looked at his colleagues for approval. They motioned with their hands for him to pull out more money. He then pulled out a $100 bill and gave it to her. She held it to the light before putting it in her G-string. Then she pulled him onto the stage and got on top of him.

She grinded on top of him, moving her body to the music as she moaned in his ear. She felt his little pecker throbbing in his pants, so she grinded harder. Tim, feeling close to being overexcited, tried to get up, but she pinned him down and grinded faster. Tim felt overwhelmed with excitement. His body stiffened and shook and his eyes rolled in the back of his head. She knew exactly what that meant. She quickly got up. And not a moment too soon. A huge cum stain started to form on the front of his pants. Both happy and embarrassed, Tim pulled $500 out of his wallet and handed it to her before rushing out the club with cheers from his colleagues reverberating off his back. Money rained all over the stage.

"Okay, who's next?"

Hands full of money flew up from all over the club.

Another song and performance later, the DJ announced her off stage. "Fellas, another round of applause for the beautiful and talented Queen Bandz and that lovely performance."

After doing a little homework, Queenie discovered Isis was working at an upscale strip club called Silk. She decided to audition and got the job. She planned to take the food right out of the mouths of Isis and Rome and put it on Boss's table.

Coming off stage and completing her rounds around the club, she stopped at the bar and ordered a drink.

"I guess Silk's is lowering their standards and becoming an equal opportunity employer if they're hiring bitches like you." Isis claimed a seat at the bar next to Queenie and sparked a cigarette.

Queenie spun around to face her. "And when you say bitches like me, you mean the kind that makes a bad bitch like you feel nervous and a rich bitch look worthless? If so, then I can see why you would feel out of place right now." Queenie cashed in some ones with the bartender.

"Bitch, you think I'm the one out of place? Nervous? I run this club. These tricks work hard all week to come see me. I'm the headliner around here. The rest of you hoes ain't shit but my opening act." A customer came over to them that Isis recognized as one of her loyal and top spenders. "Hi Walter! You come over for a dance? I'll be with you in one minute, sweety."

"Actually, I wanted to see Queen Bandz."

"Oh."

Queenie gave Isis a grim smile.

"I really enjoyed your performance. You think I could trouble you for a few lap dances?"

"It's no trouble, honey, let's go." Queenie took his hand but before leading him away, she turned to Isis. "I guess they chose a new headliner. I mean, that act of yours was getting old. Don't worry. You can be my opening act now."

She left off to the lap dance booth, leaving Isis pissed and smashing her cigarette out in the ashtray.

***

Closing time: the saddest time of the night for the customers, but it was finally a moment of relief for Cherry. She couldn't take standing on her feet a moment longer, let alone dancing. Her feet ached and everything and everyone irked her nerves, from the customers that wanted a quick feel for their dollar bills to the other dancers who beat her to customers she had her eyes set on. But the real problem was that she needed to feed the monkey on her back that she'd been trying so hard to shake.

She got her things out of her locker and when she closed the locker door, Sugar was standing there holding a bag of White Monkey in her face. "You look like you could use a pick-me-up."

"I'm good." Cherry turned to walk off, but Los was standing right behind her.

"You don't look like you're good, mami. In fact, you look sick. I don't like to see my friends sick. Sugar, give our friend here a couple of fixes on me."

"No, I-I-I can't, Los. I got to stay clean." Cherry couldn't take her eyes off the white powder as Sugar poured some on a mirror and began scraping it into lines.

"Nonsense, you need your medicine. Take it. It's the only way you will get well." Sugar blew a line, then tried to pass it to Cherry along with a straw.

Cherry stared at it for a second then reached for it, but before she could grasp it, a hand caught hers and yanked it away. Cherry looked and saw Queenie standing there holding her hand back with a fierce look on her face.

"I believe she told you no. Or is y'all asses hard of hearing?" Queenie eyed Sugar, then Los.

"She's a grown woman. She can make her own decisions. Ain't that right, Cherry?" Los stepped forward.

Queenie pulled a .22 out of her bra. In one quick and smooth motion, she had it aimed at Los's temple before he could take another step.

"Step up and get yo' brains pushed back."

Los held his hands up and stepped back. "Okayyy, mami, chill."

Sugar stood there nervously, watching the scene in front of her.

Queenie looked over at Cherry. "Let's go." Queenie then put her eyes back on Sugar and Los. "Don't ever let me catch neither one of you pushing your dope on her again. In fact, I bet' not even catch neither of you around her."

"Or what?" Los laughed.

Queenie cocked back the gun and walked up to Los and put it to his dome. "Or you find out just why I call this bitch Deuces. And I'll give you a hint: it's not because it's a .22."

Los's smile faded. Queenie eased out the door with Cherry and they jumped into Queenie's Escalade.

Silence filled the truck for the first five minutes as Queenie and Cherry drove away from the club. Cherry couldn't take the silence. She needed to know what was on Queenie's mind about what just went down and if she was going to rat her out to Boss.

"Why did you show up at the club tonight? To spy on me?"

Queenie looked over at her then rolled her eyes and stared back out the windshield. "Boss called me and told me your car was in the shop and to pick you up. He wants us to meet up with him at the club Macita and Coco working at." Queenie glanced over at Cherry again. "It's a good thing for you I came when I did."

"You know I wasn't going to give in to that shit, right?" Cherry lied, but failed to make a fool of Queenie as Queenie saw right through her lie.

Queenie shot her a look that said "yeah right". "Look, I meant every word I said in the bathroom that day at the mall. If yo' ass don't keep it together, then you know the consequences. If you need some rehab treatment or something to help you lay off that shit, then let me know and I will help you without Boss finding out. This shit got to stop. Boss's going to the top and I'm not going to have your habit be his downfall. You got me?"

"First off, I don't need no fucking rehab. Secondly, I got Boss to where he is now, not you! It was my pussy popping and grinding to put minks on his back, a Benz under his ass, and stacks in his pockets, not yours! It was me who knocked another bitch for him, not you! So you're reaping the fruits of my labor, not yours!" Cherry folded her arms across her chest.

Queenie did another quick glance at Cherry. "Well, first off…" Queenie mocked her and made quotation marks with her fingers. "Bitch, as long as you been in the game you ain't learned that a hoe can never make a pimp? Boss will always be a pimp, with you or without you. It was him that made you. It was him and his game that made you step yo' hoeing up to get those minks, Benz, and stacks. Any real hoe in this game knows that success for the family is formed by unity, by the hoes being the body and their pimp being the brain. Secondly…" Queenie mocked again with the air quotes. "You still talking minks when he has moved up to chinchilla, stacks when he's focus on millions, and Benzes when he's about to step into a Wraith. You better wake up and catch up! Or the future will leave yo' ass in the past."

King Dream

CHAPTER 14

Boss pulled into the parking lot of Club Bare Chest. A large crowd gathered outside around Break-A-Hoe, who stood next to a gray Bentley. Four beautiful women stood next to him with their heads down. Break-A-Hoe saw Boss pull up in his Benz and chuckled. Boss attempted to dial Queenie's number but before he could hit send, her Escalade rode into the parking lot and parked behind him. He stepped out of the car just as Queenie and Cherry approached and stood next to Macita and Coco.

"Sorry we a little late."

"You know how I feel about punctuality. We'll discuss y'all tardiness later. Right now, I need you bitches to deck up and be on point. I'm challenging that cat over there by the Bentley." He nodded towards Break-A-Hoe.

"If you are done prepping yo' hoes and praying that they don't go, can we please get this show on the road? The audience is awaiting." Break-A-Hoe, with most of his cheerleaders in the crowd, was feeling himself.

Polo and Princess arrived just in time to see the show.

Boss's women lined up on the sidewalk with their heads down and some feet away, Break-A-Hoe's women did the same. Amongst many other pimps in the crowd stood Pimping 6-9. Boss did his homework and found out that 6-9 was Break-A-Hoe's mentor in the game and a very well-respected pimp himself. The Bentley Break-A-Hoe stood next to belonged to 6-9. Break-A-Hoe drove a navy-blue BMW 740i .

"Ladies and gentlemen, pimps and whores! Tonight this fresh to the game stud here who calls himself Boss Bandz has challenged yours truly. Now you all don't look so appalled and applaud this player for having enough heart to challenge a pimp with as much game as I have. We all know when all is said and done, his hoes is coming home with me. And for those that don't believe let's start the show for these mothafuckas to see," Break-A-Hoe announced to the crowd. "Now player, this what's on the line. I'll give you 5 G's if you can knock one of my bitches, and when I knock one of these whores of yours, you give me 5 G's. If neither one of us knock each other's bitches, then there's no hurt to my game and no elevation to yours. You dig?"

"5 G's?"

"5 G's!"

Boss shook his head in disagreement. "Nah player, I can't do that one."

Break-A-Hoe gave Boss a quizzical look. "You telling me you can't handle dropping 5 G's?" Break-A-Hoe then turned to speak to the crowd. "You see this shit! I go out my way to give this fresh mouth-ass nigga a chance to prove his game and advance, and this nigga can't even afford the ticket to the next level!"

While the crowd laughed, Boss retrieved a small duffle bag stuffed with money out of his trunk and threw it at Break-A-Hoe's feet. "Afford it? I never said I couldn't afford it. I said I wasn't going to do it. You see, 5 G's ain't enough for what's on the line. My stable consists of nothing but thoroughbreds - I'm talking real go-getters. So 5 Gs would be neither a gain nor loss for me. I got four bitches and you have four bitches. I got 15 Gs for each bitch of mines you knock. And if for some reason, mothafucka, your mental calculator isn't working, then I'll do the math for you. That's 60 Gs on the line if you knock one of my bitches. In fact, you can have that cheese if I don't knock one of your bitches. Can you dig that?"

Whistles and excitement came from the crowd at Boss's attempt to raise the bar.

"I'm not going to put 15 G's a bitch on the line."

"Why, is that too much for your pockets?"

The sound of "ooh" being said in unison shot from the crowd.

Break-A-Hoe stepped to Boss, trying to save face with the crowd. "Nah, I just don't feel yo' bitches are worth putting such a price on their heads."

Boss thought for a split second as he nodded his head slowly, then spoke, more so to the crowd than to Break-A-Hoe. "Okay, let's go with your assumption that my bitches ain't worth such a price tag. Then let's do this, I'll put 100 G's up along with..." Boss removed all of his jewelry and tossed it onto the bag of money. "My jewelry and Benz if you can knock just one of my hoes. And all you got to do is put up your 5 G's. But since I'm putting up so much money as collateral, we have to even things out a little. So along with 5 G's, when you lose, you have to kiss the assholes of all my bitches."

The crowd got even more excited.

"Nigga, you got to be kidding me. Break-A-Hoe don't kiss no hoe's ass."

"If you say you won't lose, then you don't have shit to worry about now, do you?"

"Break-A-Hoe, put that nigga's game in the grave, baby. This nigga bluffing. He ain't got enough game in him!" 6-9 yelled from the sideline.

"Since you have so much faith in him, then I'm sure you wouldn't mind putting yo' money where your mouth is, would you?

6-9 moved through crowd to the center of the action. "Of course not. I taught him the game, so I know what he can do. So name the stakes, chump."

"I'll make it real sweet for you. If he knocks just one of my bitches, I got 50 Gs for you. If he don't knock none of my bitches and I don't knock none of his, I got 100 Gs for you. But when I knock one of his bitches, you got give me that Bentley of yours you cherish so much."

The crowd got geeked. Boss had reversed the tables on both Break-A-Hoe and 6-9. They tried to use the crowd to build intimidation in him, but instead, like an award-winning actor, Boss took to the stage and reversed the game on them. Not wanting to disappoint the crowd, both Break-A-Hoe and 6-9 agreed to the challenge.

Queenie stood with her head down, but ears open. She quickly calculated all the money Boss wagered. From what little she knew about his finances, that had to be all his savings, if he even had that much. Knots turned in her stomach - not because she doubted his game, but because of her uncertainty about Cherry's loyalty now that she was not bottom bitch anymore. After their talk on the way over, Queenie could see the amount of jealousy and hurt Cherry felt toward the bond she and Boss had. Queenie knew jealousy and pain could cause destruction. And with all that was on the line - all his money, jewelry, car, and reputation – it was enough to destroy Boss before his reign truly started.

"Well, playas, play on, and let the games begin," a familiar voice came from the crowd.

The man stepped forward and a slight smile creased Boss's face when he saw his uncle Big Hunnid step forward and spark a cigarette. Break-A-Hoe immediately went over to Boss's women and spat his game at them one by one. Boss stood there a second analyzing Break-A-Hoe's stable. After seeing what he was looking for, he went straight at each girl, whispering in their ears. Break-A-Hoe's women didn't even bother looking up at him or saying a word. Boss went back to his post and stood still with his eyes on Break-A-Hoe's stable while Break-A-Hoe continued to exercise his game on Boss's stable.

"Time's up, pimps." Big Hunnid looked at his pocket watch and blew a cloud of Newport smoke out of his nostrils.

Break-A-Hoe returned to his post. Queenie could feel the water start to fill the ducts of her eyes. To her surprise, Cherry stood strong. But seeing Boss standing alone and not with one of Break-A-Hoe's bitches told her everything Boss had worked for was now gone.

"Well, yo' hoes stand solid by you. And as you see, the concrete is stuck to my hoe's feet. So sad to say there's no advancement for you, pimp. But it's still a winning day for me." Break-A-Hoe reached for the bag of money and jewels.

Boss retracted the bag back with his foot before Break-A-Hoe could get to it. "No, no, no. Don't touch my money."

"Yo' money? Nigga, I know you ain't stooping so low as to renege on a gentleman's bet." Break-A-Hoe's hand slipped inside his jacket and rest on the handle of his .38 pistol.

Polo kept a firm grip on his heat, ready to pull and shoot if Break-A-Hoe drew his pistol. Murmurs came from all over the crowd.

"Reneging is something I'll never do. I'm a man of my word. But our bet was if you knock one of my whores or if you don't knock none of my whores and I don't knock none of yours, it's all yours."

"And you didn't knock none of mines."

"Oh, but don't be so sure about that." Boss snapped his fingers and Sapphire, Break-A-Hoe's bottom bitch, came front and center. Sapphire stood 5'6", a mulatto chick with long silky black hair and blue eyes. She had a small waist, 34D breasts, and a small bubble butt. She bowed down in front of Boss.

"I choose you." Then she pulled a stash of money from her bra and handed it to Boss.

Shock rang through the crowd.

"You disloyal-ass bitch. I was going to replace yo' ass anyway." Break-A-Hoe tossed Boss 5 G's. "You win, pimp. But it ain't no sweat to a P like me. I got three hoes that can cover the dough from one missing bitch."

"Maybe so, but I believe we still have a bit of business to handle."

Break-A-Hoe eyes surfed the crowd as he spoke. "I, Break-A-Hoe, hereby certify that Boss Bandz's pimping is real."

"That was beautiful, P, but there's still another part of our deal you must complete."

"You're not seriously expecting me to kiss these hoes' filthy asses?"

"A gentleman's bet should always be upheld by a gentleman." Boss turned to his bitches. "Y'all bitches drop them britches, bend those pretty li'l asses over, and spread those cheeks nice and wide so Mr. Break-A-Hoe can get his lips all in there."

They did as they were commanded. Break-A-Hoe gave Boss a hard mug and reluctantly walked over and one by one, put his lips in the crack of each of Boss's hoes asses. Looks of disgust and jokes against Break-A-Hoe spread from all over the crowd. 6-9 looked at Break-A-Hoe with anger and disappointment.

"You poor bred-ass nigga. You came up under me and you lost to this half-breed's low game-having-ass nigga?"

"Instead of passing insults, how 'bout you pass me them there keys and pink slip? I believe you lost too." Boss then faced the crowd. "I know y'all didn't think I was going to be out-pimped by Break-A-Hoe and this nigga who names himself after a lesbian's sex position."

The crowd laughed hysterically. 6-9 grew angry.

"Nigga, you ain't getting my car! I don't give a fuck 'bout a gentleman's bet!"

Before Boss could react, Big Hunnid stepped forward.

"Look here, 6-9, you know that's not how we playas do business. Now a gentleman's word is everything. You break the laws of the game, and every pimp in this game will lose all respect for you and make you suffer. Now are you a man of your word, or a nigga that don't deserve a gentleman's respect?"

6-9 looked at Big Hunnid then at Boss. Then he went and retrieved something out of his glove compartment. He walked over to Boss and took a hard look at him then. "Take care of her, pimp. She's always been the best hoe I had." He handed Boss the keys and title to his Bentley.

"Oh, you don't have to worry about me even driving her. I could never drive a car that belonged to another pimp. But you will still see it every time my bottom bitch drives by in it." Boss tossed the keys to Queenie. "Queen Bandz, take the keys to your new car, baby."

6-9 looked at Boss with disgust. "You giving my car to a bitch?"

"Of course. The car ain't good enough for me."

"Good enough for you? Nigga, you drive a Benz."

"Yeah, but tomorrow I'll be in a Wraith. So play catch up, baby."

6-9 felt the sharp sword of defeat and decided to walk off with his hoes before allowing his emotions get the best of him. But then Boss said something that stopped him in his tracks.

"But you know what, 6-9? There is one more hand of business we need to settle."

"And what's that?" 6-9's nostrils flared in anger.

Boss snapped his fingers and the two hoes standing on each side of 6-9 walked over to Boss and chose up.

The crowd went bananas seeing the new stud come in the game and knock Break-A-Hoe for his hoe and his mentor 6-9 for his highest breadwinners in the same night.

Polo walked over to Boss. "Bruh, you had over a 100 Gs to put up?" Boss tossed the bag of money in the trunk.

"Hell nah. More like a little more than half of that. The rest was what they call a Mississippi mitt." Boss flipped through some of the stacks of money, showing Polo cutout newspaper between the bills. "An ole skool cat I know taught me that trick when I was a kid." Boss closed the trunk and made eye contact with Big Hunnid. A smile creased Big Hunnid's face as he gave Boss a two-finger salute. Boss shot back a wink of his eye.

Queenie's nerves were everywhere. She went from nervous to relieved to excited to see Boss make such a grand entrance in the game. He came with four bitches, and was now leaving with seven. And with the way he shitted on and out-gamed Break-A-Hoe and 6-9 there was no doubt pimps and hoes would be praising his name for a long time to come.

King Dream

CHAPTER 15

Silk's song "A Meeting In My Bedroom" played as the bed squeaked. Princess moaned over and over as she felt his stiff member plunging pressure inside of her as they both got closer to their sexual release.

"Oh shit, daddy! Oh my! Oh my! Oooh, Boss!" she screamed as they both reached their climax.

Polo looked down at her. "Bitch, who did you call me?"

Princess, caught in the moment, had accidentally called out Boss's name. "What are you talking about, baby? I didn't call you anything."

"Bitch, you just said 'oooh, Boss'."

"What? Daddy, you tripping. I said 'oooh, soft'. You was going a little too hard at the end." She tried to play it off.

"You right, maybe I misheard you. I was in the moment and going hard."

"Hell yeah, you were! Come on, baby, what you thought you heard wouldn't even sound right coming out my mouth. Oooh Boss? You so crazy." Princess laughed as she got up and dipped off into the bathroom. She closed the door behind her and stared at herself in the mirror. *Damn, bitch, get it together.* While she and Polo were doing their thing, she couldn't help imagining it was Boss that was giving it to her. Ever since watching him in action the other night out-game Break-A-Hoe and 6-9, thoughts of him had been invading her mind more than usual. Even her sex drive increased so much that Polo had been having a hard time keeping up with her.

She had a lot of love for Polo, but she was starting to realize that it was Boss who truly had what she wanted. Her only choices were to either choose up to Boss or find a way to shake him off her mind and heart before things got bad.

While Princess was in the bathroom preparing to get in the shower, Polo searched her purse and phone for any signs of her messing around with Boss or any other man. He'd been having trouble trusting her lately. He had noticed the side glances she was always giving Boss and the extra friendly demeanor she had towards him. He knew something had to be going on between them. He just hadn't found the evidence he needed yet. All this madness has been causing him to drink more than usual and become possessive of her. He even made Princess stop hoeing and only work the clubs. He didn't want another man inside of her.

Polo's search got interrupted by the ringing of his phone. He tossed Princess's phone on the bed and answered his. "What!"

"What? Did I call you at the wrong time or something, P? Why all the hostility in your voice?"

Polo plopped down on the bed and placed his hand on his head. "Nah, I'm just a little tired. What up though?"

"I know the feeling. I could use a little rest myself. Did you know some of the people in the crowd outside the club the other night took video of the challenge and uploaded it? Polo, the video went viral." Boss was excited.

"Yeah, superstar, I heard."

Boss could almost feel a slight hint of jealousy in his voice. "Superstar? Well, if I'm shining, you shining too, baby. Like the fly told the other fly over dinner, we in this shit together. So with that in mind, I was thinking we should take our act on the road while it's still hot. I'm talking cross-country pimping. You down for this tour?" The phone went silent for a second. "Polo?"

"Yeah, I'm down."

"Good Then get some sleep with yo' cranky ass. We leave for Chicago in the morning."

Polo hung up the phone and reached for the bottle of Crown Royal on the nightstand.

A cross-country tour with Boss was the last thing he wanted to do. He wanted to keep Princess as far away from Boss as he possible could, especially after the game he displayed the other night. If he could take them bitches so easily from two well-known pimps like Break-A-Hoe and 6-9, then he could easily peel Princess from his grasp. And Polo wasn't having that. He agreed to the tour with the hopes that they could make enough money so that he could buy his own barbershop and for Princess to get out of the game and they could settle down. He wanted her all to himself. He figured all he had to do was just keep her away from Boss until the tour was over.

Even though she swore to the heavens nothing was going on between her and Boss, Polo could almost feel it in his heart that was a lie. He could almost swear to it that he heard her say Boss's name in bed. Soft and Boss don't sound shit alike. But then again, it could just be his paranoia.

***

After leaving Chicago, they headed to Indianapolis, then Lexington, Nashville, Memphis, and then Atlanta. So far, the cross-country tour had been a success. Pimps showed Boss so much love in every city they went to. That video had his name ringing bells all over. Even his women were given the VIP treatment everywhere they went. That alone made them want to hustle even harder for him. It was of no doubt to him now that he had unlock this next level of the game.

He got inside his hotel room to find all his women inside. "All my women in one room. We must have something dire to talk about. What seems to be the problem?"

Queenie stepped forward. "There's no problem, daddy. Me and the girls have a little something for you." She snapped her fingers and the women lined up side by side. One by one, they bent over and hiked up their skirts. Each had a tattoo with Boss's name going across their ass cheeks. Around his name were $100 bills with his face instead of Benjamin Franklin's. "We wanted to show our loyalty and dedication."

"Is that right? Then let's see yours."

"I was saving the best for last." Queenie bent over and removed the long shawl from around her waist. "Queen Bandz" is what read across her ass with the same $100 bills with Boss's face on it. But the bills continued down her legs and in between her thighs. Then she turned around and removed her shirt. On her chest read Forever My Heart And Soul To Boss Bandz with a portrait of Boss seated on a throne. "You like ?"

"I never seen a more beautiful sight. But I hope them asses ain't too sore to receive daddy's loving."

"Absolutely not. And if they were, it ain't nothing wrong with a little pain and pleasure," Stormy, the former bottom bitch of 6-9, chimed in.

"Then let's have a little fun." Boss stretched across the bed and his women swarmed him like bees to honey.

With lust for Boss on her mind, Coco forgot she had Princess on hold. But Princess didn't mind as she listened to the moans, screams, and squeaking of the bedsprings. The sounds of ecstasy coming from the other end of the phone made her soak her panties. She wanted to hang up, but she couldn't. The sound of Boss's voice as he commanded his women around the bedroom with so much dominance gave her chills of excitement. Her pussy throbbed with desire. Her hand slowly crept between her legs. She slowly massaged her sweet spot, making her juices rain down even harder.

"Daddy's dick feel good to you?" she heard Boss say to one of the women but she couldn't help but answer him herself.

"Yes! Daddy's dick feels so good!" She squeezed her breasts and nipples as she massaged her clit faster, letting the phone rest between her ear and shoulder as she chased her nut. Before she could get there, she heard Polo slide his key card into the door. She quickly ended the call and placed the phone on the nightstand and tossed the covers over her head before he walked in. *Damn!* she screamed inside her head as her pussy remained wet, throbbing, and unsatisfied.

Boss's women laid spread out on the bed and floor, trying to catch their breaths. Coco's phone rang. The Megan Thee Stallion song "B.I.T.C.H." was the ringtone that played. It let Coco know just who was calling. "Daddy, could you get that for me? It's Princess."

Boss picked the phone up off the table and answered it. "What's up, li'l mama? Hello?" The other end remained silent a few seconds, then hung up. "Her phone hung up."

"She must've pocket dialed by accident again. If not, she'll call back." Coco was too tired to get up and call her back herself. Boss had drained her of all her energy.

***

Stepping out of the shower, Boss overheard a bunch of commotion outside the bathroom door. He wrapped a towel around his waist and before he could reach the door, Macita came rushing in.

"Papi, come quick!"

Boss, sensing the urgency in her voice, pushed past her and into the other room. All the girls were crowded around somebody on the floor.

"What the hell going on?" Boss walked up closer to the scene.

Queenie looked up at him. "Daddy, it's bad."

Boss looked down at the woman Queenie was kneeing in front of and saw a bloody and battered Princess. Her face was swollen to almost twice its usual size. Her nose was broken, lip busted, and both eyes swollen. Scratches and handprints decorated her neck. She cried hard and tried even harder to catch her breath. It hurt with every breath she took.

"Boss, we need to take her to the hospital. She's in bad shape."

"No! No hospital," Princess protested.

"Coco get some towels and y'all clean her up. Princess, you calm down and tell me exactly what happened."

Princess sat up and took a few deep painful breaths to calm herself. Then started talking. "Lately Polo's been having it in his head that you and I are messing around."

"Why would he think that?"

"I don't have a clue. It's been driving him to drink a lot more than usual lately. And when he drinks, he gets worse. He's so paranoid that he made me stop hoeing. He wanted me to stop dancing too, but I told him I wasn't until I have enough money to retire. So he comes to work with me every day and babysits me. He had it in his head that we would make enough money on this cross-country

tour that I could stop dancing and live a white picket fence life."
Coco and Queenie gently nursed her wounds.

"But why did he snap like this tonight?"

"He made a run to the liquor store while I was asleep. I happened to wake up when I heard the door close. I got up to call Coco so I can borrow a few things of hers."

"Oh my God, I forgot I left you on hold." Coco put her hand over her mouth.

"So I hung up and laid back down. Polo walked in a moment or so later. He said he saw the screen on my phone was lit up on the nightstand so he knew I wasn't asleep and that I had just got off the phone. Anyways, we got into a full-blown argument about who I was talking to. I showed him my phone and he seen the call log said Coco. He left it alone for a minute and went to his bottle. I thought all was done and over with. But then…" Princess hissed as a sharp pain shot through her lower abdomen.

"You okay?" Coco put a hand on her back.

"I'm fine. But then I'm in the bathroom getting ready and he comes storming in slapping me and throwing me against the wall. Saying that wasn't Coco I was talking to, it was Boss. He said he called the number back and you picked up the phone. He said he knew we were messing around and all type of crazy stuff. The more I tried to convince him he was wrong and it was all in his head, the more he beat me. When he got tired, he grabbed the keys to my truck and left me bleeding on the floor. I'm sorry, Boss, I didn't know what to do, so I came here."

"Her bath water is ready." Gemini, the other woman Boss knocked 6-9 for, said from the bathroom doorway.

"Bitch, fuck a bath. Everybody pack up and let's go!"

"Daddy, what's wrong?"

"Queenie, this ain't no shady motel we're staying in. And the way he just beat this bitch, somebody had to hear it. If not, them cameras had to catch her coming down to this room all bloody. So it won't be long before Johnny Law comes knocking at this door, and that's not good for business. Now get this bitch up and out of here. We're going to check into another hotel on the other side of town. Now move it!"

The women dispersed to their rooms quickly to gather their things and load up. Coco and Queenie helped Princess to her feet. As soon as she stood, blood rushed down her thighs and a sharp pain in her stomach nearly knocked her back down.

"Oh my God, Boss!" Coco was on the verge of tears at the sight of her friend.

"Get her to the hospital Now!"

"Boss, I can't move. It hurts too much."

"Shit!" Boss snatched the blanket off the bed and wrapped her in it. He carried her to Queenie's Escalade and laid her across the backseat. Coco hopped in the back with her and held Princess's head in her lap. She tried to comfort her as much as she could. Queenie hurried into the driver's seat and started the engine. "You remember seeing Grady Memorial Hospital when we first got into town?"

"Yes!"

"Then get her there now!"

Queenie smashed off and Boss hurried back inside to finish packing. It definitely wasn't the kind attention he needed on this trip. And he definitely had to holla at Polo about the sucka attack he had before things got any more out of hand.

King Dream

CHAPTER 16

Three days had gone by and still no word from Polo. But a source had tipped Boss off to where he was staying.

Boss pulled up to the rundown motel in east Atlanta where it was said Polo was laid up at. He knocked on the door, but got no answer. He was sure he was at the right place because Princess's truck was parked in front of the room door.

A couple of doors down, a maid came out of one of the rooms. Boss whistled to get her attention. He nodded his head towards the door and imitates a key turning the locks, signaling for her to unlock the door for him. She shook her head no and continued placing items on the cleaning cart. He whistled again. This time he flashed a $50 bill at her. She glanced around before coming over, snatching the money, and unlocking the door. She pointed her stubby finger at him. "This never happened."

"Agreed."

Boss walked into the room. Clothes, fast food wrappers, and empty bottles littered the floor. An episode of *Spongebob Squarepants* played loud on the TV. He turned the TV off. Polo laid passed out on the bed. Boss walked over and kicked the bed hard. "Polo, get up!" Polo groaned, but didn't move. Boss grabbed the ice bucket off the dresser that was half filled with melted ice and threw it on him. Polo immediately jumped up out of bed.

"WHAT THE FUCK! Boss? What the fuck you doing here? And how the hell did you find me?" Polo picked his shirt up off the floor and wiped the water off his face.

"I haven't seen or heard from you in three days. Not since you left that bloody, battered bitch of yours crawling down the hall to come knocking on my room door. Putting me and my family's lives and livelihood at risk. And all you can say is what am I doing here and how did I find you?"

"You know, the proper thing to do is say thank you when some-one gives you a gift."

Boss couldn't believe that even Polo could find humor in such a serious situation. "You call leaving a half-dead bitch on my doorstep a gift?"

"It don't matter what shape the gift's in. It's the thought that counts. And I was thinking of you with every blow I gave that bitch." Polo laughed as he picked up a bottle of gin off the nightstand and turned it up. "You wanted her; now you got her."

Boss was starting to get pissed off with Polo's attitude, and it was taking everything in him to not beat some sense into him. "What the fuck are you talking about? I never wanted her."

Polo threw down the shirt he used to wipe his face with. "Don't lie to me! Don't you dare lie me! The least you could do is respect me enough as a man not to lie to my face! I seen the way the two of you look at each other and how y'all act with each other."

Boss could see the game was already fucking Polo's head up. "You have seriously lost your fucking mind! I tried to warn you this game ain't for everybody. And I knew this game wasn't for you."

"Why? Because you're afraid I would be better than you?"

"What the fuck is you talking about? This has nothing to do with being afraid of you being better than me. Look at you! You turning against your own nigga for a bitch! A bitch I had no desire for. That ain't pimping. You're like my brother! I would never steal food off your plate or a bitch off your dick."

"You think I believe a word that's coming out your mouth?" Polo took another swig from the bottle. "Nigga, we ain't friends, we ain't brothers, we ain't shit! Fuck you!" Polo turned the bottle up again and this time, he spit it in Boss's face.

Boss punched him in the jaw, then threw him into the wall. He snatched the bottle out of Polo's hand and threw it against the wall on the other side of the room. The glass shattered everywhere and the liquor bled down the wall.

"That's your fucking problem! You letting that damn bottle talk for you. The only reason I'm not putting my foot off in yo' ass right now is because I know you're drunk and don't mean shit you saying or doing!" Boss held him against the wall by the collar of his shirt.

"A drunk man's words is a sober man's thoughts. I meant every word I said. You ain't shit to me. And I wouldn't mind never seeing your ass again. In fact, I prefer that. From now on, stay the fuck out my life Boss!"

The words shot through Boss's heart with the pain of a silver bullet to the heart of a werewolf. The look in Polo's eyes gave confirmation to every word he said. Boss couldn't do nothing but respect his wishes.

"A'ight." Boss let him go both literally and figuratively. He wiped his face with the sleeve of his shirt as he walked to the door. He opened the door and looked over his shoulder at Polo. "I'm going to leave you with this update on Princess. Three broken ribs, a fractured eye socket, torn blood vessels in both eyes, and a broken nose."

Polo smiled to the verge of laughter at how he had ruined her. He knew she would no good to Boss now.

"Yeah, champ, you really did a number on her. But you know, that wasn't even the worst of it all. All that damage you done to her is what caused her to lose the baby she didn't know she was carrying. Your baby! Yeah, that's right, you killed your own child."

Polo's smile began to fade and his face weakened with sorrow. Boss had never seen a look of more hurt on his face than he had seen just then. He pulled a piece of paper out of his inside jacket pocket and placed it on the chair next to the door. "Here's the title to the truck. She said you can keep it and she never wants to see you again."

Boss then walked out so he wouldn't have to bear witness to the tears that were threatening to fall from Polo's eyes. As he closed the door behind him, he also felt the closing of that proverbial door to their relationship. He knew not having his best friend in his life would be a hard change to adjust to, but there was no choice but to adjust. As they say in show business, The Show Must Go On.

***

Balloons, teddy bears, and get well soon cards filled the room with sympathy, which in turn reminded Princess of all she lost and made her that much more depressed.

She learned early on how to use her beauty as currency. Even as a kid, people worshipped her good looks. Her mother used take her to the store and people would comment on how beautiful she was and buy her whatever she wanted. When she became a teenager and her body blossomed, men went crazy for her. They dug deep in their pockets for whatever made her happy. Her looks were everything to her. And now they were gone. She felt ruined. She couldn't look in the mirror anymore without breaking down at the sight of the hideous creature that stared back at her.

She laid in the hospital bed with her mind constantly reeling over the day she lost everything. No matter how many times she replayed the turn of events over and over in her head, the rivers of tears never ran dry. Her mind was slipping deeper off into a state of depression when a sudden knock at the door took her mind away before those rivers began to overflow once again. "Go away!" she yelled with her back facing the door. But the door opened anyway. "I said I don't want to be bothered!"

"Not even by me?"

At the sound of his voice, she quickly sat up. "Boss? What are you doing here?" She wasn't expecting him to come see her. It was hard for to conceal the excitement of him being there. But then she suddenly realized he could see her. He could see her hideous face. She quickly turned her head to try to hide her face.

"I wanted to come check up on you."

"Oh, you didn't have to do all that. I'm fine."

"They treating you alright in here?"

"Yeah. The doctors say I'll be fit to leave in a couple of days."

Boss walked over to the other side of the room to admire the gifts from the gift shop that the girls had been buying her. Princess turned the other way to dodge his view of her.

"So I hear. What do you plan on doing when you get out of here?" Boss admired a Tweety Bird card that Macita gave her.

Tweety Bird always reminded him of his mother. Her high yellow skin had earned her the nickname Tweety.

"I guess I'll be going back to St. Louis to live with my granny until I get on my feet. Find me a nine-to-five or something." Princess fiddled with the hospital band on her wrist.

"You don't sound too happy with that."

"I don't have much of a choice."

"I hear you. I want you to know I talked to Coco and she told me what you wanted me to tell Polo. I took care of that business for you and gave him the papers on the truck."

Fear shot through Princess, almost making her turn around and look at him. "Boss, you didn't tell——"

"No, relax. Everything's all good. Listen, I'm going to get up out of here. I got a lot of business to get together before me and the girls leave Thursday." Boss headed for the door then stopped. "But you know, the craziest thought just struck me."

"What's that?"

"How about instead of you going back to St. Louis, you come with us and finish out this tour?"

Princess's face lit up for the first time since that dreadful day. She couldn't believe Boss still wanted her around with the way she looked. But she still didn't dare look his way. She didn't feel fit to look into his face, let alone be in his presence.

"Boss, I can't. Look at me. The doctors say it could be months, if ever, before some of these wounds are to heal. And I still may be left with some scars and visual damage. A trick ain't going to pay a battered bitch like me significantly enough to keep you fed. I'll just be taking up space that could be used for a girl that's more worthy."

"I appreciate you trying to look out for what's best for me and my business. But let me worry about that. Anyways, I was thinking more on the lines you being like my assistant. Run errands, placing ads online for the girls, answering phones, booking their dates, and shit like that. To be honest, it was all Coco and the other girls' idea. You know, even though you and Polo ain't together, them hoes still see you as family."

"And what about you?"

Boss walker over and turned her face towards him and planted a kiss on her forehead. "Me? I'll be here in two days to pick you up. Let that be enough said."

Boss then left the room leaving Princess with a smile on her face and a newfound hope in her heart.

CHAPTER 17

All the hoes of the top pimps in Milwaukee gathered in Rome's kitchen to drink, smoke, and gossip while the men did the same in the front room.

"Girl, let me tell you. Silky took us to Las Vegas for a week and I made my man 4 G's!" Tiny, the newest girl to Pimping Silky's stable, bragged as she showed pictures in her phone of the trip to Las Vegas to the other girls.

"4 G's? That's all you made in a week? Where the fuck was you working, Fremont Street?" All the women laughed. "I know of crack whores who can make that in a day out there. It's no wonder why yo' man still drives a Jaguar that's four years old."

Isis's teasing deflated all the pride out of Tiny's chest and shrunk her with embarrassment. Isis turned to Peaches. "Where my bitches Stormy and Sapphire at? Now them hoes know how to hustle."

"I haven't been seen them, 6-9, or Break-A-Hoe lately."

"Y'all ain't heard?" Heather, a snow bunny belonging to Pimping Top Notch, chimed in.

Isis poured some champagne and orange juice in a glass. "Heard what?"

"This new stud challenged Break-A-Hoe and broke his ass off for Sapphire. Then the slick-ass nigga knocked 6-9 for his two top breadwinners, Stormy and Gemini, and took his Bentley."

"Bitch, you got to be lying. Stormy wouldn't leave 6-9 for shit in the world. And you telling me 6-9 lost his Bentley to this cat? I call bullshit."

Heather pulled out her iPad and pulled the video up then handed it to Isis. "See for yourself. The whole thing went viral. I don't see how you don't know about this already."

All the girls who hadn't seen it crowded around Isis to get a view of the video. The video began. Isis saw the familiar faces of pimps and hoes she knew. She saw Break-A-Hoe jacking to the crowd about how he was going to humiliate some new stud that wanted to challenge him. She watched a Benz pull up and when she saw who stepped out, her eyes widened with shock.

"I know him. That's Boss Bandz. Me and Peaches ran the Charlie on him and his boy Polo some months back. I know you ain't telling me this is who knocked them?"

"Yup," Heather replied.

The girls continue to watch the video. Some of them laughed at how Boss took over the show and how he made Break-A-Hoe kiss the assholes of all his whores.

"Heather, has Rome seen this yet?"

"Peaches, Top Notch is showing it to him now in case he hasn't. That new cat Boss is talking about coming for the crown."

"That mothafucka ain't got what it takes to remove Rome from the throne! Y'all pimps is supposed to be the next best thing to my man and they couldn't even knock him off the throne. You think this new nigga, this nigga that has no respectable mentor in the game, could knock him? Get y'all minds right if that thought ever came across your minds." Isis's blood had started boil at the thought of Boss taking the throne. But at the same time, she couldn't help but admire his game and swag. He put on quite a show.

In the other room, Rome rolled up a $100 bill and blew a line of powder, then another, before passing the tray to a pimp next to him. He pinched the bridge of his nose and sniffed before leaning back in his chair and resting his arms on the armrest. "Yeah, I seen the video. 6-9 and Break-A-Hoe should be ashamed of their fucking selves. They didn't deserve them hoes, the dough, or that damn Bentley for letting that young stud's game out-slick them like that."

Fleetwood Slim, Rome's right-hand man and number two pimp in the game, stirred the ice around in his glass. "His name has been ringing a lot of bells lately. And word is he's coming for the crown."

Rome leaned forward and looked Fleetwood dead in the eyes. "Nigga, you say that like I should be worried. And I'm trying my hardest to figure out why the rest of y'all ain't laughing at such a joke." They all began to put on their best fake chuckles to kiss Rome's ass. "Now you may think this cat can out-pimp all of you. But it's the greatest joke ever told if you mothafuckas is to ever believe for one second that he could out-pimp me." The face Rome made looked mean enough to scare a bulldog.

"Of course we don't believe for one second that this stud could do such a thing. I was just giving you the word on the streets, baby." Fleetwood passed Rome the tray of cocaine.

Rome put the $100 bill back to work and vacuumed up four lines this time. He then leaned back in his chair with his head to the ceiling while the other pimps laughed and conversed about other shit.

Rome had to admit Boss displayed some damn good game. He couldn't believe that was the same cat he and the girls Charlied some months back. And Rome couldn't help but notice that there was something familiar about the young cat's swag. He just couldn't quite put his finger on it. He didn't believe Boss could take the throne, but he knew Boss was somebody he had to keep an eye on in the game, or anything could happen.

***

After being on the road for the past ten months, Boss and his team had reached the final city of their tour. The Los Angeles sun shined bright and the ocean breeze gave a sense of tranquility to both Boss and Princess as they sat on the beach going over business and upcoming events.

"Okay, Boss, you say we got two months to play out here. So what's your plan?"

Over the months, Princess's wounds had healed and her confidence started to increase little by little. But the scars left on her face made her too insecure to work. Boss didn't mind keeping her around because she always proved her worth. She made sure the girls kept a busy and organized schedule, ran errands, and did whatever Boss told her to. She did everything possible to prove herself to be an asset to the family. Since picking her up from the hospital, she and Boss grew closer and even became intimate. She even had confessed to him how she always had a desire for him when she was with Polo. He was reluctant at first to take things to that level with her because of his love for Polo. Then he realized Polo was no longer in the realm of his loyalty, so he gave in to the possibilities of what could be. And when she gave birth to Li'l Boss, it further tied their bond.

"Princess, you don't have to worry about being my assistant anymore. I no longer desire those services from you."

"You quitting me?" She put her head down so he wouldn't see her cry. "I can't say I didn't see this day coming. I just held out hope that it wouldn't. I don't blame you though. I can't produce like the rest of the girls, so there's no need to keep me around. Don't trip. I'll pack me and Li'l Boss's things and be on the next flight out of here."

"Pack? Bitch, I ain't telling you to leave. I'm telling you I don't want you to be my assistant anymore. I don't need you being my assistant. I want you back in the game where you belong. You miss it, don't you?"

Relief ran through her body. She couldn't stand the thought of not being without Boss. He was everything she ever wanted in a man. "Of course I miss it. But Boss, I can't work with these scars on my face and my nose looking the way it does."

"I knew you would say that, even though when I look at you, I see beauty both inside and out. So to get you to see what I see, three months ago I decided to call up the best plastic surgeon in the United States. And he happens to be right here in L.A. And you have a consultation with him in about thirty minutes."

So much excitement filled her that she didn't know what to say. "Are you serious? What about Li'l Boss?"

"Don't worry about Li'l Boss. Me and the girls got him while you heal up. So get yo' ass in the car and let's go before we be late."

With a huge smile on her face, they hopped in the car and rode out. His fame was growing strong and he was getting closer to the crown. It wasn't time to relax in his newfound star status. It was time to grind even harder. Time to pull out every trick up his sleeve and every hoe at his disposal. It was time to put Princess to work and milk her for all she was worth.

CHAPTER 18

After being on the road for over a year, Boss and his team were finally back home. His reputation grew to extraordinary levels. His bank account was starting to read like the numbers on a scale a whale sat on. There was no doubt he now had the money and respect. Now all that was left was to seize the throne to get the power.

He walked into G's Clippers, the barbershop where all the pimps hung out at and got trimmed up. As soon as he stepped inside, he was greeted with recognition and respect from all the pimps there. The head barber kicked a client out of his chair to service him. Boss sat down for a fresh shave and lining. Him and the other P's spent the next 45 minutes conversing about the latest haps and some of his experiences on tour.

The barber finished his shave and lining. Boss went to check his fresh in the mirror, then hit the barber's hand with some extra scratch to show his satisfaction. "Alright, fellas, as usual, it's always a treat when players meet. But before I get up out of here, I need y'all to spread a word til it reaches the bird I need to fly my way."

"What's the word, Boss?" Pimping Silky asked.

"I hereby challenge Rome for the throne. Any place, anytime."

"Boss, I dig yo' ambition, baby. But you know the counsel has to vote you worthy enough to challenge the king. And even before that could happen, you have to first take the number two spot from Fleetwood Slim."

"Since when did a pimp have to be number two before he could take the number one spot?"

"About five months ago, Rome brought the suggestion to the board and we had a meeting on it. And we all agreed that it should be the proper way of doing things."

Boss felt disappointed, but not defeated. It was just another obstacle in his way. "Answer this for me. If y'all going to agree with everything the king says, then why the fuck do we have a committee?"

Everyone remained quiet, not knowing how to answer Boss's question without looking like suckas.

"Well, if that's the way it's got to be, then you tell Fleetwood if he got the balls and the game, then I challenge him. Saturday, I'll be at Club Rain. Make sure everyone's there. Because if he doesn't show or he turns down my challenge, then I want everyone to see the fear I put in his ass so they'll know who is truly the king."

Boss exited the barbershop and headed home.

***

After a passionate session of lovemaking, Boss and Queenie laid in bed sweating, trying to catch their breath. "You trying to wear a pimp out or something?"

"I'm just trying to keep up with you."

Boss kissed her on the lips. "Well, you doing a good job." Boss got out of bed and went searching for something in the closet.

"What you looking for, daddy?"

"I got something for you."

"You got me a gift? Don't play with me, you know I love presents."

Boss found what he was searching for, then walked towards the bed with his hand behind his back. He sat down next to Queenie on the bed. Queenie quickly sat up, eager to see what he had for her.

"Close your eyes." He moved his hand from behind his back and held the gift in front of her. "Alright, you can open them." Boss opened a little black box and Queenie had a picture-perfect look of surprise on her face. Her hands covered her mouth as she stared down at the diamond ring.

"Is that what I think it is?"

"Look here, baby, you understand me and I understand you. We been too much in sync for too long for this not to be forever. So this is me making a promise to you of what will be in store for you once we get to the top. You with that, baby?"

She nodded her head, still in shock. "Yes!"

Boss placed the ring on her finger. She wrapped her arms around him and kissed him passionately. And before he could protest, she had him lying on the bed for another round of love making.

***

After a couple days being in town resting up, Boss took the girls out to Club Rain. Club Rain being a more upscale and exclusive club, only the people who are somebody or with somebody that's somebody could get in. It was the spot for celebrities, kingpins, mafia bosses, politicians, major pimps, and the elite. It was where those at the top of the food chain go to mingle, make new connects, and have a good time.

Boss and his team claimed their seats in VIP. The women talked amongst each other about who's who in the club. Meanwhile, Boss was scanning the club for Fleetwood Slim. He saw many of the other pimps, but no sign of Fleetwood. Hoping Fleetwood would show up to accept his challenge was the whole reason Boss had even come out. He knew if Fleetwood showed up, Rome would be there to watch the event. And if Boss was to beat Fleetwood, he would challenge Rome in front of every elite individual in the club. So if Rome was to turn him down, his reputation would shatter in every direction.

An hour and a half went past and still no sign of Fleetwood or Rome. The girls took to the dance floor, leaving Boss solo.

Cherry walked over and sat down next to him. "That's a nice ring Queenie's sporting. Does it mean what I think it means?"

"If you are asking if it's an engagement ring, then yes." Boss wasn't really in the mood to have that conversation with Cherry at that moment. Not while he was already frustrated with Fleetwood not showing up. It wasn't the proper time to deal with Cherry's attitude, but he knew it was best just to get it out of the way. "Bitch, just go ahead and say what's on your chest so we can get this shit over with and enjoy the rest of the night." Boss turned to face her direction. But to his surprise, there was no hostility on her face, only sadness and streams of tears running down her cheeks.

"I don't know what to say, daddy. It's all my fault. If I hadn't fucked up and gave up my position, that could've been me. I made you stop loving me."

Boss had no choice but to cater to her emotions. He put an arm around her. "Stop loving you? Cherry, baby, I never stopped loving you."

"Then why her and not me?"

He figured he would have to eventually answer that question for her. "Queenie's been in my life since we were kids. But you don't have to be in competition with her. Because what me and her have don't take away from what you and I have. You understand me?" She nodded her head in agreement. "Good. Now let's dry these tears so I can enjoy that sexy smile of yours." A smile started to return back to her face. "There it is. You know, it was that very smile there that made me have to have you when I first seen you."

"Is that right? You sure it wasn't that money you seen me stuffing in my bra?"

"Oh, it was most definitely that too."

They both busted out laughing.

"Boss, I love you. I got too much of me invested in you. And I don't want to lose you. You feel me? So promise me, daddy, that this won't change what we have together."

"Cherry, baby, I promise as long as you don't change on me, I'll never change on you. And our commitment to each other will be just as strong as the commitment Queenie and I share." Boss leaned in to kiss her.

Before his lips could touch hers, the moment got interrupted by someone clearing their throat to get his attention. Boss spun around and saw Rome standing next to him.

"I wasn't interrupting nothing was I...pimp?"

Boss made a gesture with his head to let Cherry know to move around and let the men talk.

"Not at all. But where's that ass kisser of yours, Fleetwood? Out parking your car for you? Tell him to take the night off. They got valets here for that. So let's get down to business."

"You got a lot of tongue, young stud."

"That's funny, yo' bitch say the same thing."

"Maybe you should think about showing the king a little more respect."

"The king? Nigga, I'm the king. You're just a nigga in the way. And once I take your man Fleetwood out the game, I'm coming for your ass."

"You think a nigga like you could dethrone me? Nigga, just before I walked up, you were about to lip lock with that whore of yours. I could never fall to a nigga who tongue wrestle whores."

"Yeah, I kiss my bitches. Sorry to hear that disturbs you. But I give a fuck less about how unorthodox it may seem to you. You see, to keep my money coming, I put my foot up my hoe's asses when they fuck up. And I love them like they want to be loved when they make me proud. I guess that's why I got more hoes on my team than you. Now quit the bullshitting and tell yo' mans I said let's get this show on the road."

"Well, pimp, I'm sorry to tell you, but your dreams of becoming number two will have to be put on hold for just a little bit. Our dear friend Fleetwood ran into a few legal woes and won't be available for at least another six months or more. So I thought I would come down here to deliver the bad news myself. Didn't want you to feel like he was dodging you or anything."

Boss slammed his hand on the table in disappointment.

"Don't worry, young P, you'll get your chance." Rome grinned, but before walking off, his smile faded when he saw a familiar ring on Boss's hand. "Where did you get that ring?"

Boss saw that he was referring to Cadillac Bandz's old ring. Besides the Holy Bible Of Game, it was all he had left of his pops.

"Oh, this here? It looks familiar to you? It's a fascinating story behind this here ring." Boss held his hand up and admired the ring himself. "You see, it once belonged to a great king. And when that king passed away, it was given to his prince along with a lot of game so that the prince would take over the throne and become king. But first, the prince had to dethrone a great deceiver in order to grant his father's dying wishes. But by hell or high waters, the prince will be sure those wishes be granted."

Rome then realized Boss was going to be a lot more trouble for him than he originally thought.

"Well, playa, we all have our missions in life. You enjoy the rest of your night. And thanks for the bedtime story." Rome tipped his hat to him, then made his exit out the club.

Boss was fuming. He was ready to get Fleetwood out of the way. But deep down, he knew Rome was going to try some underhanded bullshit to prevent that. Boss seeing Rome's nerves rattled by finding out who his father was further showed him that the game he inherited was too much for Rome to compete with. The smell of that fear in Rome was like the taste of blood to a wild dog for Boss. He wanted more. Rome might've bought some time with Fleetwood being locked up, but not much. Boss was determined to find a way around that. Rome was going to face him in a challenge one way or another.

CHAPTER 19

Boss placed Li'l Boss in his swing, then kicked back on the couch. He was busying himself scrolling through his emails when his phone rang. "Hello."

"Hello, Boss."

Boss thought he recognized the voice, but there was no way it could've been who he thought it was. "Who is this."

"It's Isis."

It was exactly who he thought it was. "What the hell you want?"

"We need to talk. It's important."

"Well, talk."

"Not over the phone. Can you meet me somewhere?"

Boss didn't like the sounds of it. It all had the makings of a setup. "Tell me what this is about before I agree to anything."

It was obvious to Isis that Boss didn't trust her. And if she wanted him to meet with her, she had to make it good enough for a man to want meet with the main bitch of his enemy. "It's about something Rome has planned against you. I'm quite sure it's something you need to hear."

Boss knew Rome was going to come after him the closer he got to the throne. So whether true or not, Isis aroused his curiosity. "You got my attention."

"Meet me at the Suburban Motel at 3:30 this afternoon."

Boss checked the time on his Audemar watch: 1:56 p.m. "I'll be there."

The call ended.

***

Curiosity had gotten the best of Boss, without a doubt. But his curiosity didn't come without caution. He arrived at the motel 45 minutes early. He parked across the street from the hotel in the K-Mart parking lot, laid low in the cut, but with a good view of the motel without being seen.

Twenty minutes had gone by when an Uber car pulled in front of the motel. Out hopped Isis in a Nike sweat suit with matching hat. She wore shades to help conceal her identity. After paying the driver, she walked into the office to secure a room. She came out and checked into room 27 on the south end of the motel. Another ten minutes went by and she rang Boss's phone to check if he was he nearby. Boss told her he was a few minutes away. He hung up and continued to watch the motel a little while longer. Fifteen minutes and two missed calls later from Isis, Boss's was satisfied no one else would be showing up to this meeting to surprise him. He pulled into the motel parking lot and tucked his Glock 40 in his waist. He went up to the door just as Isis was coming out. He caught her by surprise, nearly scaring her heart right out her chest. She quickly shielded her fear with attitude when she saw that it was Boss.

She put her hand on her hip. "Oh, now you show up?"

"You asked for my time. I didn't ask for yours. So you get it when I give it."

Not having the words to come back at him with, she smacked her lips give off more attitude.

"Come inside before someone sees us together."

Boss walked in behind her and locked the door. Isis tossed her hat and sunglasses on the bed. Then she plopped down on the mattress and lit a cigarette. Boss took post against the long dresser that an old tube TV sat chained to. Boss looked around the room at the stained carpet floor and its early 90's furniture and décor. The room smelled of sweat and stale cigarettes.

"You want to tell me why a pampered bitch like yourself got us meeting up in this dump?"

"Because it's the last place Rome or anyone else would think I would ever be."

He could see the logic in that. Indeed, no one would ever expect her to be slumming it.

"Makes sense. Now what is it that Rome has planned for me?"

Isis puffed on her cigarette and dumped the ashes in a plastic McDonald's cup. "Last night, Rome came home drunk. I overheard him on the phone with Fleetwood. He was saying something about you being the son of Cadillac Bandz. Then he got to speaking about you knowing things that could put an end to him. He was so upset. I've seen Rome do some gruesome things. I even seen him face the most frightful situations with a smile on his face. But until last night, I've never seen him more nervous and afraid of anything ever. So whatever it is you know is terrifying enough that it scared the devil to church this morning."

"He has every reason to be afraid. Now tell me what he has planned."

Isis took another long pull of her cigarette and released the smoke out her nostrils. "Five months ago, after hearing your name ringing bells all over and hearing about your reputation of embarrassing pimps you challenge, Rome felt you might try to get too big for your britches and try to challenge him. So he went to the counsel and demanded that a law be drawn up saying in order for pimp to challenge the king, he must defeat the number two pimp first."

"That ain't shit new to my ears. The counsel already informed me about the new law and the author behind it."

"But that ain't all. The other day, word got around to him that you indeed was coming for the crown and you was ready to get Fleetwood Slim out the way. Rome wasn't ready for you to have that opportunity, so he planted a small amount of dope in Fleetwood's car and tipped off one of his detective friends downtown."

"You saying he set up his own right-hand man?"

"Yes. He knew Fleetwood wouldn't get much time off it. But he also knew it would be a good way to stall you from challenging either of them."

"That dirty mothafucka that afraid of me? What is he buying time for?"

"All I know is he told Fleetwood it's time the cat scratches the kitten."

The term was familiar to Boss. It was a term used by ole skool players when they were about to make a serious move on a young player.

Boss meditated on it for a second. Isis put her cigarette out in the cup and nervously sparked up another one. Boss, not able to suffer another breath of her cancer sticks snatched it from her then dropped it in the cup.

"That's enough of those. Tell me, why is Rome's loyal bottom bitch coming to warn me about all this?"

"I want to know what it is you know about Rome that's got him on edge?"

Boss knew the bitch had to have some kind of angle. "You want to know for you? Or did he send you to find out what all I truly know?"

Isis got off the bed and walked up to Boss. "What, you think I'm here to spy? I want to know for myself, Boss. I want to know what it is you could possibly have on him that got him so shook up!"

"That's between me and him. All you need to know is that he's not who you think he is."

"That's not good enough."

"Well, it's going to have to be." Boss turned to leave.

"Tell me, damn it!" Isis grabbed his arm to stop him.

Boss out of reaction, gripped her arms and pushed her against the wall. Both their faces were tensed with anger. But his mood softened as he looked into her beautiful green eyes. At that moment, he found that irresistible desire for her he had when he had first seen her walk through the doors of Club Rave. Before he knew it, his lips were on hers and their tongues were dancing the tango on the dance floors of each other's mouths. The sexual tension between them exploded. Their bodies slammed against the walls and dressers as their sexual desires grew more and more intense. Their clothes came off, flying all across the room.

He was aware that he would be getting in the bed with the devil, literally, if he were to sleep with Isis. But he still jumped right into those proverbial flames. She moaned, squirmed, and squeezed the sheets until her knuckles turned white as he entered inside of her. Her tight wet velvet walls squeezed his member as he stroked her with vengeance. Boss removed his belt, then flipped her around doggy style and wrapped the belt around her neck like a leash.

"I ain't forgot about that Charlie shit. So since you acted like a bitch that day, I'm going to fuck you like one today." He pulled the belt tighter as he slid back inside her.

She cringed and screamed with pleasure as he stroked her mercilessly. He went too deep and she tried to crawl away. Boss snatched her back by the ankle and slapped her on both butt cheeks, then pulled her hair as he shoved his member back inside her. Then he put his mouth next to her ear. "Bitch, don't run from me run to me!"

The combination of his motion and his display of authority and control over her along with the discipline he put on her activated a volcanic eruption between her thighs. Boss felt her walls tighten as she began to erupt. He pulled her hair and thrust himself deeper inside of her, plunging her flower with long, hard strokes as her nectar began to flow. She threw her head back and screamed as loud as she could. Then, feeling all the energy drain from her body, she fell flat on her stomach.

Isis turned over and saw Boss getting dressed. "Leaving already?"

"I got business to take care of."

"What about filling me in on what you got on Rome?"

Boss paused, getting dressed. "So that's why you gave that ass up to me? Thinking that was going to get me to tell you what the dirt is I have on him?"

"No! It ain't shit like that."

"Then why? Was it because you're ready to choose up?" Isis suddenly broke eye contact with him. "Hmm, like I thought. Let's put it like this so we both feel okay about what just happened. You gave me some good information. And I gave you some good dick. The way I see it, fair exchange ain't robbery. It's just business. I'll see you around." Boss chucked her the deuces before leaving the motel room.

A beeping sound from her purse let Isis know she had a missed call. Retrieving the phone from her purse, she saw she had more than one missed call. She had seven missed calls, all from Rome. "Shit!" She called an Uber and hurried back to her hotel room.

She got to her room and all seemed quiet. But when she closed the door, a hand grabbed the back of her neck.

"Bitch where the fuck you been!" Rome's grip on the back of her neck was so tight that it sent pains down her spine making her lose her grip on her purse and all its contents came spilling out onto the floor.

"I went for my afternoon run."

Rome yanked her back, making her fall backwards onto the floor. "Hoe, don't you dare lie to me. I seen you hop out that Uber. Now where the hell you been?"

Isis slowly eased away from him and scooted towards the bed. "Rome, I went for my run baby. You know how I get sometimes when I'm too deep in my thoughts. I run a little too far out. So I caught an Uber back. Daddy, look at me, I got on my damn jogging suit. I only went for a run."

"Then why you ain't been answering your phone?"

"I had my earbuds in and didn't hear it ring."

Rome was aware that Isis's way of clearing her mind was to go running. And sometimes she would wander off so far in her runs that Rome would have to come get her. Sensing what she was saying could be the truth, he gave her the benefit of doubt.

"You know all you had to do is call me and I would've came and got you." Rome helped her back up.

"I know. I didn't want to bother you. You seemed to be having a lot going on lately."

"A lot has been on my mind as well."

"Want to tell me about it?"

"Bitch, no! A pimp can handle his own mind. You go in there and get cleaned up and stay focused on hoe business."

Isis hopped in the shower, letting the hot water rain down her body, her mind and body still reeling with all the pleasure Boss put upon her. She couldn't believe she fell so far into his arms. But she held no regrets for what had transpired between them. Confusion built in her heart and mind. She knew, no matter how much she denied it, since the day she met Boss, she felt a special connection to him. The wreckage left back at the motel from their sexual escapade was proof enough of it. She'd been in the game long enough to know Boss wasn't just fucking her for the sake of a nut. He was conquering her, almost making her give in and choose up. But her love for Rome remained the crown of her heart.

Before she could unravel all her thoughts and feelings, the bathroom door burst open. Rome snatched the shower curtain open.

"Out jogging, huh, bitch?"

Isis almost collapsed to the floor with fear when she looked at what Rome held in his hand. She couldn't believe she remembered to erase all her calls to Boss and take an Uber to a shady motel on the other side of town, but forgot to ditch the key card and motel receipt for the room. There was no lying her way out of that one. She was no doubt in for a world of pain.

King Dream

CHAPTER 20

Boss awakened the next morning to the buzzing of his phone vibrating on the nightstand. With his head pounding like a mad drummer, he reached for the phone. "Hello."

"Good morning."

Boss blinked his eyes hard to try to adjust them to the bright sunlight shining in from the open curtains. "What do you want, Isis?"

"I need to see you. I got something for you that'll make your day."

"Look, bitch, I shook your bed once. And shame on me for not being faithful to my pimping. So it won't be no more of that. I'm a pimp bitch, not a sugar dick player looking to trick his dick off for a fat ass and cute face."

"I'm not calling you to come tangle my sheets, Boss. We need to talk. I'm at this bar lounge inside the airport. Meet me here." She ended the call.

Boss got dressed and drove to the airport to meet up with her.

***

When he arrived, the sounds of smooth jazz playing inside the lounge gave a sense of calm within its doors, which made it feel like heaven after leaving all the noise and rush of people outside its doors. Boss's eyes scanned the bar and found Isis sitting with luggage at a table far in the corner. He walked over and took a seat at the table. Isis's face lit up at the sight of him.

"It's nice to see you again."

"I'm sure it is. So what's this, your attempt at taking me out on a date?" Boss joked.

"Straight to the point, I see."

"Time is money."

"In that case…" She pulled a manila envelope out of one of her Gucci luggage bags. She slid it over to him.

"What's this?" He opened it up to see it filled with crispy $100 bills.

"20 G's."

"I can see that. But what is it for?"

The server came over to their table. Isis ordered them drinks and sparked a cigarette.

"I'm choosing up."

Boss tried to keep a straight face, but couldn't hold back his laughter.

"You choosing up? Mrs. Rome, the woman with concrete feet, choosing up? This got to be a joke. You really want me to believe your pampered ass is willing to go from being Rome's bottom bitch to just another whore in my stable?"

"It's the truth!"

"Why? Why would you give all that up?"

Isis's eyes rolled behind the tint of her shades. She was becoming agitated trying to convince him that she was indeed serious. "You know, most pimps wouldn't ask so many questions. In fact, they would kill each other over the invitation to have me in their stable."

"And that's one thing that separates the king from all the rest. Now, you care to answer my question?"

Isis exhaled hard, then removed her shades and revealed her swollen black eye.

"That's quite the shiner you got there."

"It looked a lot worse a few days ago."

"What happened?"

Isis put the shades back on and took a puff of her cigarette. "When I came back from the motel that day you and I met up, Rome was waiting for me. I had missed several of his calls and he was pissed beyond belief. I told him I was out jogging, but that only bought me a few minutes time. He busted into the bathroom after finding the motel receipt and key card. He dragged me out the shower and beat me until I told him who I was with."

"You told him you was with me?"

"I'm still alive, ain't I? I told him I went to kick it with some dude from out of town that I met at the club. I told him I had tricked some pussy off to the nigga and that it wasn't nothing serious."

"Then what happened?"

She sniffled and removed her shades, then used a napkin to dry her eyes. She returned her shades back to her face before continuing.

"Then he took off his belt and beat me some more. He took me home, took my phone, and locked me in my room for the past five days. He stayed home, making sure I didn't get out. But today, I guess he had something important to take care of because I heard him leave the house for the first time since. And as soon as I heard his car pull out of the driveway, I immediately packed as much as I could as fast as I could. Then I came here and called you."

"Did you ever think what you would do if I chose not to accept you? What would you do, go back to Rome?"

"No. If you reject me, then I'll walk over there and buy a one-way ticket out of here."

Boss analyzed Isis searching her body language for any signs of deception. With Rome in fear of losing the throne to him, it was hard for Boss to trust anything Isis said.

"So what do you want me to do?"

After a second of weighing the situation at hand, Boss got up and started to walk off, making Isis's heart sink in her chest. He stopped and looked over his shoulder.

"If you coming home with me, then you better put that cigarette out and bring yo' ass and my money."

"Yes, daddy."

Together, they exited the airport and headed to the four-plex apartment building where Boss housed Cherry, Coco, Macita, Stormy, Sapphire, and Gemini.

***

The small brick apartment building was close to the airport and in a pleasant Oak Creek neighborhood. It was a perfect spot for the girls to catch johns coming and going out of town who wanted a quick nut.

Boss and Isis entered the building and could hear loud music coming from apartment one and knew where to find the girls. When they entered the apartment, Sapphire was sitting on the floor Indian style in the front room going through a box of CD's. Stormy was in the bathroom mirror curling her hair. Gemini practiced pole tricks in the front room on a portal pole. The rest of the girls huddled around the computer, checking out YouTube videos of other strippers. Queenie happened to be there checking on the girls when he and Isis arrived and he could tell she wasn't too happy to see Isis by his side.

"What the fuck this bitch doing here?" Queenie instantly got dirty looks from Sapphire and Stormy. "And what the fuck you bitches looking at? What you brought this bitch here for?"

"Queenie! I understand your concern. But bitch, you better find yo' hoe manners and think twice before ever questioning me again." Boss gave her a stern look.

Queenie sat back down and Boss addressed the team.

"Now I know it's some bad blood between some of you and Isis, but that shit ends today. She's team Bandz now. And I expect for each and every one of you to treat her like family." He looked deep in each of their faces as he spoke. "Do I make myself clear?"

All the women agreed.

"How do we know we can trust this bitch?"

"I didn't ask you to trust her. I'm telling you to trust me. And if I say she's good, then she's good. Any more questions?"

Queenie folded her arms across her chest and pursed her lips.

"Then welcome her to the family."

The women approached Isis one by one gave her a hug and warm welcoming. When Queenie's turn came around, she walked over with a fake smile plastered on her face and gave Isis a hug, then whispered in her ear.

"Look here, bitch. I know your snake ass is up to something. Know that I will be watching. If I find you trying to bring this family down, I'm going to take my Glock 9 and I'm going to knock your noodles right out your bowl. Okay?" Queenie kept a bootleg smile on her face as she spoke. She broke their embrace and addressed the other girls. "Ladies, let's pop the champagne and celebrate. Y'all know how we do when this family grows. So let's party and toast it up."

They grabbed the champagne and toasted to Isis.

Isis's phone rang and Boss could tell by the nervous look on her face as she stared at the caller ID that it had to been Rome calling.

"I'll take that." He took the phone from her.

All celebration came to a halt as all the girls watched as Boss put the call on speakerphone.

"Well damn, nigga, you must have ESP or something. I was just getting ready to call you."

"Boss?"

"The one and only."

"You got to be shitting me! Where's my bitch?"

"You ain't got no bitch over here, player. If you were referring to Isis, I hate to give you the blues on that news, but what you had with that hoe is through. She chose up to me." The line went silent a moment. "Caller, are you there?"

"We tried to spare your young ass. Now you're going to have to face the consequences."

"Who do you mean by we?"

The other end of the phone went dead.

What did Rome mean by we? Was he referring to him and Fleetwood? The pimp council? Who? He wanted to let his mind wander more on the subject, but he had more pressing matters that deserved his attention. He made a call he thought he'd never had to make.

"Hello?"

"What's going on, chief?"

"Boss?"

"Yeah, it's me."

"Hey, it's a surprise hearing from you."

"I know. Remember you told me if I ever needed anything to let you know?"

"What can I do for you?"

"I got a friend that could use some help."

"Say no more. Meet me at the station and we'll talk."

"I'll be there in an hour."

A champagne bottle popped just as he ended his call. The girls were in full celebration mode. He could see some of their joyful faces were genuine and others were imitations. He knew his decision to accept Isis into his fold could be a good thing and a bad thing. With the original team being at odds with Isis and the hoes he knocked from Break-A-Hoe and 6-9 being tight with her, it could either add to or divide his family. But he was determined to make it work. Like a true mack, he was going to pimp it to the end.

***

Fleetwood inhaled a deep breath of freedom before jumping into the limo that awaited him outside the Dodge County jail. His women welcomed him inside. After being around a bunch of hard legs for the past weeks, he couldn't be happier to see their beautiful white faces. "Daddy's home, ladies! Yeah, and I know y'all missed me."

The three snow bunnies hopped all over him. He was all smiles and having the time of his life as they devoured him. They pleasured him until his eyes rolled in the back of his head and he met his release.

The partition came down. "Alright, bitches, that's enough. Now let daddy handle some business with Mr. Fleetwood," Boss said from the driver's seat, disguised as a chauffeur.

The three women moved away from Fleetwood and sat closer to the partition.

"What the fuck is this?" Fleetwood quickly buckled up his pants.

"Isn't it obvious? I knocked you for your whole stable. And with that, there's no need for me to challenge you to knock you out of the number two spot, according to the rules of the game. Now don't look at me like I'm a bad guy. As you see, I was nice enough to pull some strings to get them to drop the case against you. And I let you play in them pink pussies one last time. But you want it again, you going to have to pay."

"You dirty son of a bitch!" Fleetwood started to charge Boss through the partition.

Boss pulled out a Desert Eagle and pointed it dead at him. Fleetwood stopped in his tracks.

"Come on now, player. No need for violence. This here is a non-contact sport, baby." Fleetwood eased back. "Now what I want you to do is get yo' ass out the car."

Fleetwood looked outside the windows. "Get out? We in the middle of nowhere."

Boss cocked the gun back and aimed it at his head. "Your problem, not mine."

Fleetwood got out of the car. Boss sped off before he could finish slamming the door shut.

Fleetwood looked around at the countryside and farm animals in the fields on the side of him. Then he saw the limo come speeding back in reverse. His hopes went up that he won't have to walk back to civilization.

The limo pulled beside him and Boss rolled the window down. "Oh yeah, you tell Rome I said game's over. I'm coming for that throne." Boss then sped back off.

Fleetwood kicked the tail end of the limo as it jetted off, leaving him in a cloud of dust.

King Dream

CHAPTER 21

Cherry sat alone in her room, whispering on the phone. "Just make sure yo' hittas know to leave no room for a miracle."

"That's no issue. You just make sure you have my money."

The call ended and Cherry tossed the phone on the bed. Even though Boss told her things between them wouldn't change, she still felt things would never be right unless she got rid of Queenie for good.

She picked up her purse off the nightstand and pulled out her pocket mirror and a bag of White Monkey. In the middle of blowing a few lines, she heard her bedroom door creak. She hurried to hide her dope under the covers. "Who is it?" She wiped visible residue off her nose with her hand. No one answered back. Far as she knew, she was home alone. Everyone else had business to take care of, leaving her home alone. She had things to do too, but not for another hour or so.

She went to the door opened it and peeped both ways down the hall and didn't see anyone in sight. Satisfied she was just tripping, she closed the door and got in the shower.

Getting out of the shower and walking back into the room, she noticed the door was slightly ajar. She could've sworn she closed it. She peered down the hall again and again there was no one in sight. The house remained quiet. She picked up her mirror and poured out some more White Monkey onto it. She formed two fat lines to get herself right for the day. With straw in hand, she dived right into one of the streaks of powder. She instantly felt a burning sensation in her nose as the first line made its way down her nasal passage. "Goddamn! Los made this mix too strong." She blinked her eyes rapidly and squeezed the bridge of her nose. She regained her composure and dove in to polish off the last line. She snorted the last line as fast as she could to power through the burn.

Then it all hit her at once. Her whole world started to spin faster and faster. She fell back on the bed and everything went black. All she could hear was the sound of her heart beating slower and slower.

Then there was nothing. Everything went quiet. And Cherry was gone.

***

Boss and the girls watched as the gravediggers lowered Cherry's pearl white casket into the ground. There were no tears in his eyes, but his heart still pained the same. He peered down at the hole in the ground that would become her eternal resting place. He kissed a pink rose he held in his hand, then tossed it on top of her casket. He said his goodbyes, then he and the girls got into the limo and left the cemetery.

Boss sat quietly watching life go on outside the limousine window. He couldn't believe Cherry was gone. He cursed himself for being so oblivious to her addiction. He wondered how he did not know she was on that stuff. He couldn't help but feel like it was all his fault, thinking the pressure he put on her had to drive her to it. Why she couldn't tell him what was going on was all he could wonder.

Though his Maybach shades concealed his eyes, Queenie knew behind the tint of those glasses was a fountain of pain ready to rain from his eyes. She laid a hand of comfort on his shoulder.

"Baby, you okay?"

Boss said nothing and continued looking out the window.

Queenie sensed he didn't want to be bothered and decided not to press him any further. "I'm going to leave you alone. Just know we're here for you if you need us."

Those very words had gotten Boss's attention. "Here for me?" Boss face frowned up at her. "To be there for me also means to be there for each other."

"We know, daddy. That's what family is supposed to do." Queenie rubbed his hand.

"Well, where the FUCK was y'all at when Cherry was putting that shit up her nose!" Boss pounded his fist against the limo door, making Queenie jump. "You bitches wasn't there for her. And you supposed to be my bottom bitch, but you want to try to convince me you didn't know she was on that shit? You knew. And the reason why you didn't tell me is because you used it as leverage to knock her out of position so you could become the bottom bitch." Queenie put her head down as it weighed heavy with guilt and shame. Boss rolled down the partition. "Stop the car!"

The driver pulled over and Boss opened the door.

"Boss, don't leave!" Queenie cried, but the only response she was given was the door slamming in her face as he left.

Boss made tracks to the closest bar he could find. He got to 34th & Auer Street and walked into People's bar. He sat down at the bar and welcomed the smooth burn of whiskey down his throat. His mind thought back to all the good times he and Cherry had. She was his hoe and he had a pimp's love for the bitch, a love deep enough that it made him feel like a piece of him was missing, but yet shallow enough that he couldn't shed a tear.

As he drowned his sorrows in whiskey, a short, thin Cuban woman copped a seat next to him and sparked up a Black & Mild cigar. Her attention completely focused on him.

"You Boss Bandz, right? You was Cherry's man. I seen you get out the limo and I followed you here. I'm Lulu, by the way."

Boss turned to get a look at the woman. Her jittery demeanor, Rudolph red nose, and bad case of the sniffles gave Boss all the signs of a powder junky.

"Sorry, sweetheart, you ain't my type. Clean yourself up, and maybe then we can talk." He slammed a shot of whiskey and gestured for the bartender to bring him another round.

"I'm not here looking for you to be my pimp."

"Well, I'm not a dope dealer baby or looking for a sympathy fuck. So what is it that you want?"

"I was a friend of Cherry's. We danced together at Club Paradise. I followed you here because I got some information that you might want."

"What kind of information?"

"It's regarding who's responsible for Cherry's death."

Boss's glass stopped short of his lips. He called the bartender back over to him. "Bartender, get my friend here whatever she likes."

Lulu ordered a Long Island iced tea.

"Alright, li'l mama, you got my attention."

She drank a swallow of her Long Island before beginning. "Cherry was copping White Monkey from this dealer named Los. Los serves all the girls in the club. He has a bitch named Sugar who works at the club. Sugar turns out all the girls she can on White Monkey for him. Then once the girls opens up Pandora's box, Los starts slipping heroin in the mix."

"To keep them coming back."

"Exactly. A few girls had overdosed before off his mix, so he had turned it down a little."

"Then what? He accidentally put too much in the mix Cherry had?"

Lulu drank some more of her drink, then a took a hard pull of her Black & Mild. "What happened to Cherry wasn't no accident." She exhaled a cloud of smoke and dumped her ashes in a nearby ashtray.

"You saying they killed her? What makes you say that?"

"Cherry had gave up White Monkey after surrendering her position as bottom bitch to Queen Bandz. But the night you challenged Break-A-Hoe, Los and Sugar tried to push the shit back on her. Cherry tried to reject them, but they kept trying to push the shit on her. Cherry would've caved in if Queen Bandz didn't show up when she did."

"Queenie showed up?"

"Yeah, she showed up, all right. She pulled her gun out on Los and told him and Sugar if they were to ever come near Cherry again, she would blow their brains out."

"Then what?"

"Cherry and Queen Bandz left. Los was furious and was saying something about those bitches going to get what they got coming and them bitches are dead." Lulu saw the anger in his face grow as she spoke.

"What all do you know about this soon-to-be dead man?"

"Everything. Even things Sugar doesn't know about him. One night, I was turning a date with him and he was wasted and started rambling off at the mouth about his whole life. He told me everything!"

Boss pulled out couple of hundreds and slid it her way.

"Then you fill me in with all you know."

Lulu slid the money back towards him. "I'm not doing this for the money. Cherry was my friend and I want to see those son of a bitches pay for what they done to her." Lulu's eye began to water and Boss could see the hurt in Lulu's heart for losing Cherry.

Lulu unloaded all the information she had on Los to Boss. Meanwhile, Boss was forming a plan in his head as she spoke. When the conversation came to an end, he got up to leave.

"I know you say you didn't tell me this for the money. But I'm sure Cherry would want you to have it anyway." He slid the money back to her and left.

***

An Uber car dropped Boss off at home a little after one in the morning. After leaving Lulu at the bar, he went and put a few other things of business in line. He opened the door to the four-bedroom home in the suburbs where he, Queenie, Princess, and Li'l Boss lived.

The house was quiet when he walked in. He went upstairs to Li'l Boss's room and found him and Princess asleep in the rocking chair. He walked over to take Li'l Boss from her. Princess awakened when Boss took him out of her arms. "Shhh, go on to bed," Boss told her before she could say a word.

Exhausted by the day's events and Li'l Boss, she didn't even put up a fight. She went straight to her room and crashed. Boss laid Li'l Boss in his crib and turned on the baby monitor, then went to his room.

Queenie laid in bed asleep. Boss sat down at the edge of the bed and began removing his shoes. Even though he tried to be as quiet as possible, he still had awakened Queenie. "Boss, you're home. Thank God. Baby, I'm so sorry." She hugged him from behind.

"I know."

"Daddy, you was right. I did know she was using. And I used that to get her to step down. But I told her she would have to stay clean or I was going to tell you. She promised she would stay clean. And ever since then, she was clean! I don't know what made her relapse. Baby, I swear if I had any signs she was back on that shit, I would've told you."

Boss patted her hand. "I know. And I know why she relapsed."

The pain on Boss's face made Queenie shed tears as he told her about his and Cherry's conversation that night at Club Rain. Once they were done shedding their emotions, Boss held her in his arms and until they fell asleep with the hopes that tomorrow would bring them a better day.

***

Rome and Fleetwood sat in South Ridge mall getting their shoes shined. Fleetwood was still sour about losing his stable to Boss, and so was Rome.

"We got to do something about Boss, Rome."

"You're preaching to the choir. That son of a bitch is a lot slicker than I thought. I heard one of his whores overdosed."

"Yeah, that bitch Cherry. But that ain't slowed him down. That dirty hand bastard already secured the number two spot. It's not gonna be long now before you have to face him for the number one spot."

The shoeshine boy did one final shimmy on his shoe, then slapped his shoes with the rag. He was all done. The shoes shined like a fresh dime. Rome stood up.

"I have no worries on that. Boss won't be taking my place. I got something planned for his ass that's going to stop him in his tracks. Just wait and see."

Rome tipped the shoeshine boy a twenty. Then he sent a text message on his phone that put his plan against Boss into motion. There was no doubt to him that his plan was gonna knock Boss out of the box for good.

CHAPTER 22

Sugar sat on the couch watching soaps in her nightgown when the doorbell rang. She opened the door and there stood the mailman. His eyes was stuck on her big breasts that were busting out the top of her nightgown. She saw where his attention was and closed her robe and cleared her throat. "What, you never seen tits before?"

"I'm sorry, ma'am. I have a package for a Cindy Rothschild."

"That's me."

He passed her the package and the electronic clipboard.

She signed and handed it back to him.

"You know, if you ever need——" Suga closed the door on him before he could finish his lame attempt to get in her pants.

"I hope this is Hollywood offering me a movie script." She reclaimed her seat on the couch and examined the thick envelope. There was no return address. She opened it up and her heart could've stopped at what she saw. "YOU DIRTY MOTHER-FUCKER!" She flipped the coffee table over and commenced to destroying the living room in her fit of rage. "That son of a bitch is going to pay for this!" She dropped to the floor, breathing hard. She sat with her back against the couch. Then picked her phone up off the floor and made a call.

"Hello, Hector? My name is Sugar. I think we need to talk."

***

A few days later, the doorbell rang. Sugar got up and answered it.

"What the fuck is so important that I had to come right away?" Los said, walking through the door, pushing past Sugar.

"You might want to go in the kitchen. I fixed you up something real nice."

"I'm not hungry," Los told her but still took the path to the kitchen. When he walked in, his heart almost exploded when he saw the two men standing there and the man seated at the kitchen table.

"Hello, Carlos. Long time no see." The man seated spoke with a gentle voice and a strong Spanish accent.

His heart went in his throat and his eyes nearly popped out his skull when he seen the table full of the money and kilos he had stolen from Hector. Los turned to Sugar.

"What did you do?"

Sugar leaned against the kitchen entrance, holding the envelope the mailman delivered to her a few days ago. She tossed it over to him.

"I told you from the beginning, motherfucker, not to ever fuck me over."

Los opened the envelope. It was filled with pictures of his wife and kids and a copy of their marriage certificate. But what really put the nail in his coffin was the copies of recent text messages between him and his wife. The messages were updates and how close he was to ditching Sugar and getting the money they needed for a new life. He found it hard to swallow. His throat had never felt so dry.

Los had robbed and killed Hector's nephew for 25 bricks of cocaine and heroin and blamed one of Hector's rivals, which turned the streets of Mexico into a bloodbath while he skipped town. To boost his repertoire of a bad ass, he told Sugar all about it. Now all his sins had caught up to him.

"Sugar, this is yours for your help." Hector slid her two bricks of coke and five grand cash. "And for you, Carlos, we're going to take a long ride."

The men grabbed Carlos and dragged him outside kicking and screaming. He was loaded into the trunk of Hector's rental and never seen again.

***

Days were starting to look a lot brighter for Sugar. After getting rid of Los, Sugar got herself a real agent. This particular morning, he gave her the call she had been waiting her whole life for. She was selected to be one of the lead characters in a horror movie she auditioned for a few days ago. Even though they weren't due to start shooting the film for another month, Sugar was so excited she decided to pack up right then and head for California.

She tossed her luggage into the trunk of her Jaguar and stuffed the two kilos of coke she got from Hector in her purse. She figured she could make a little money and mingle with the powder head celebrities when she got there.

She jumped in and started up the car, ready to put Wisconsin in her rearview for good. But before she could put the car in reverse, someone sprang up from the backseat. They put a hand over her mouth and a straight razor to her neck. Her eyes sprang open wide with shock as she stared into her attacker's face in her rearview mirror.

"I know you didn't think you was going to walk away from this free and clear. You killed my friend. Now it's your turn to meet the reaper. Tu blanco puta morir! (Die, you white bitch!).

Lulu then carved a smiley face across Sugar's windpipe. Sugar's body jerked as her blood sprayed all across the windshield. She bled out within seconds. Her eyes remained wide open, staring out into nothingness as there was no life left in her. She was dead.

Lulu slammed Sugar's head against the steering wheel as she pushed the driver's seat forward and hopped out of the car from the backseat. She popped open Sugar's purse and cuffed the two bricks of coke and cash. She pulled the hood of her hoodie over her head and faded out of scene and into the city streets.

***

Coming from the car wash after getting his pearl white and powder blue Wraith shined up, Boss headed to the tailor to pick up his wedding tux. Now that Fleetwood was out of the way and having the number two spot, Boss was certain that he was going to take the throne from Rome. With that certainty, he and Queenie decided to go ahead and have their wedding.

Isis had been with him three months so far and had been proving to be more of an asset than a burden. On her worst nights, she was bringing in $1600. She was cashing him out daily by the purse load.

Coco and Macita even began to warm up to her. Queenie still didn't trust her. But out of love and respect for Boss, she kept her personal feelings harnessed.

With less than a month left to the wedding, Boss still hadn't elected a best man. He even attempted reaching out to Polo with the hopes that they could put their differences behind them. But Polo had changed his number. His only other option was his uncle Big Hunnid.

The stop light turned yellow and Boss sped up to make it. But before he could get halfway through the intersection, the light turned red. Almost two blocks past the intersection, red and blue lights flashed behind him. He pulled over. Two officers got out of the squad car and approached his car from both sides. The short and stocky Mexican officer approached the passenger's side while the other officer, a white man with red hair and freckles, approached the driver's side.

Boss rolled down the window. "Good afternoon, Officer."

"You mind telling me what's your hurry there, sir? You blew past that red light like NASCAR driver."

"I'm sorry about that. I got a wedding coming up and I'm running late picking up my tux. And with all the stress of wedding planning with the wife-to-be, the last thing I need is for my her to be jumping down my throat about not having my tux."

"I can understand that. I just got married myself."

"So you feel my pain?"

"Most certainly. I tell you what, give me your license and registration and as long as you don't have any outstanding warrants, I'll let you go with a warning."

"Sounds like a good deal to me. Here you go, Officer." Boss gave him his license and registration.

Both officers went back to the squad car to run the check.

A few minutes later, they came back to Boss's car with their guns drawn.

"Mr. Bandz, step out of the vehicle," the Mexican officer ordered him as he cautiously approached the passenger's side.

"What seems to be the problem, Officer?"

"Step on out here and I'll explain everything to you in a second," the other officer told him as he opened Boss's door.

Boss stepped out of the car and was immediately placed in cuffs. "I need to know what's going on and why I'm being placed in handcuffs?"

"Mr. Bandz, there's a major warrant out for your arrest."

"Warrant? For what?"

"For rape and battery, asshole!" the Mexican officer told him.

"What! Hell nah! That has to be a mistake. Look at me, does it look like I have to rape a bitch?"

"I'm sure you can get it all sorted out downtown. So watch your head and take a seat." The freckled face officer helped him into the back of the squad car.

"What about my car? Can I at least call my wife-to-be to come get my shit?"

The officer called Queenie for him and informed her of the situation, then told her where to pick up Boss's car.

***

Boss sat impatiently in a room at the downtown police station, waiting for a detective to come talk to him. His gut told him Rome had to be behind all of it. He also wondered if Isis could be in on it too.

His thoughts got put on pause when a short, fat, blonde hair lady walked in. "Hello, Mr. Bandz, I'm Detective Frances. I'm sure you're wondering why you are here."

"You damn right I am! The fucking cops said something about a rape and battery. I ain't rape nobody!"

"But you did beat her, is what you're telling me?"

"Hell no, I didn't do none of that shit. I don't even know who the hell y'all talking about I'm supposed to had did something to."

Detective Frances picked up the file sitting in front of her. She opened it and began to read from it. "It says here the victim's a 24-year-old African American female named Nisha Jones, who also goes by the alias Peaches. Says the suspect, Boss Bandz, made many offers to take her out. Said the suspect was a frequent customer of hers at Ricky's Gentlemen's Club, where she worked as an exotic dancer. Ms. Jones states each time suspect Bandz offered to take her out, she declined. On the afternoon of April 19, 2020 at approximately 1:35 p.m., Mr. Bandz showed up at Ms. Jones's apartment, forcing himself in. Suspect Bandz then proceeded to beat and rape Ms. Jones, forcing her to perform such acts as giving him oral sex and inserting foreign objects into her vagina. The victim then states this went on for over an hour."

Boss couldn't help but laugh as loud as he could uncontrollably.

"Mr. Bandz, this is no laughing matter. You are looking at some serious time here. We're talking at least 10 to 20 years in."

Boss turned red with laughter. He then calmed himself down and let her in on the joke. "You should tell this alleged victim of yours to do their homework before they go around making up stories. There's no way I could've done this. It's physically impossible for me to be in two places at once."

"What do you mean?"

"I mean, you say this took place at 1:35 p.m. on April 19th. At that exact time, I was actually here. Between the hours of 12:15 to a little past 3:30, I was here waiting to post bail for a Ms. Carla Carrillo. You can check your cameras right now if you think I'm lying. And that's all I've got to say before my attorney comes down here and exposes the incompetency of this department." Boss leaned back in his chair and clasped his hands behind his head.

Detective Frances picked up the phone and made a call. "Hi Tracy, this is Detective Amber Frances of the special victims unit. I need you to tell me if you had a Boss Bandz come in on the 19th and place bail for a Carla Carrillo. Oh, you do remember him? Yes... Okay, thanks Tracy." She hung up the phone. "Well, Mr. Bandz, we owe you an apology. Your story checks out. You're free to go."

Boss gratefully exited the room. He was glad he didn't have to call the chief for another favor. He found it ironic how bailing Macita out after getting busted with a stash of weed is what helped bail him out.

After retrieving his belongings, he proceeded to leave, but was stopped by the sound of his name being yelled. He turned around to see police escorting his whole team to booking -everyone except for Princess, Isis, and Queenie.

"Coco, what's going on?"

"Boss, I swear we didn't do anything. We were downtown getting things together for the wedding when these two jackasses..." She nodded her head at the two detectives who arrested them. "...arrested us on prostitution charges. When there's no proof of us doing nothing more than shopping!" Coco said, yelling more so at the detectives than talking to Boss as officers escorted her into a holding cell.

"Where's Queenie and the other girls?"

"They had to go to the bakery and check on the wedding cake."

"Look, y'all, don't talk and don't trip. I'm going to bail y'all out of here ASAP."

Boss walked away to the elevator. He knew there was of no use talking to the detectives that brought them in. It was obvious Rome had them in his pocket.

"After this wedding, I'm going to take care of Rome once and for all," he said to himself as the elevator doors closed. And he meant every word of it.

King Dream

CHAPTER 23

The small church held about 40 guests, mostly Queenie's people. For Boss, he had his mother and some close friends of hers, along with a few of his. Boss stood at the altar looking stunning in his all-white Ferragamo tux along with freshly-lined goatee and crispy braids. His groomsmen stood beside him in all white tuxes with lavender trim. His groomsmen consisted of Big Hunnid as his best man, and the three other men were his cousins Big D, Wayne and Baby G. He never kicked it with them much throughout his life to feel close to them. Baby G was always in and out of jail since he was a juvenile for doing dumb shit. Big D was always a square. He went to church faithfully every Sunday and had been waking up to the same bitch every day since high school. Boss could in no way, shape, or form relate to the two of them. But Wayne was the cool one. Boss actually wished he could spend more time with Wayne. But Wayne's life was just as busy as Boss's was. He owned nightclubs in Atlanta, California, and Miami. He lived a bachelor's lifestyle and knew all about making money. Boss could definitely relate to that.

Tina stood at the altar as Queenie's maid of honor while the girls stood next to her as Queenie's bridesmaids. They wore all-white silk dresses with lavender trim, matching the groomsmen.

Boss stood at the altar nervously as the organist began to play the ceremonial Here Comes The Bride song. A moment later, Queenie came walking down the aisle in her all-white silk Ferragamo wedding dress. The site of her eased Boss's nerves. He felt it in his heart he was doing the right thing by marrying her. There was no other woman in the world who deserved to have forever with him more than she did.

There wasn't a dry whore's eye in the entire church after Boss and Queenie exchanged the vows they had written each other. They kissed, and for the first time ever were introduced as Mr. and Mrs. Bandz. Then everyone left the church and traveled to the reception hall to get the celebration started.

The bride and groom took a seat after much dancing. Tina danced over to their table. "Congratulations, you two!" She reached over to give her sister and new brother-in-law a hug. After a few seconds of conversation, Tina walked off and Queenie turned to Boss.

"Baby, this is the greatest day of my life."

He kissed her lips. "Mines too, baby." He raised his champagne glass. "To us, and what is now forever." Their champagne glasses kiss as they toast and took a sip. Queenie leaned in to whisper in his ear.

"I got something special for you when we get to Fiji."

"Oh yeah? What's that?"

"It's a surprise. So you will have to wait until the honeymoon to find out."

Boss couldn't wait to see what she had in store for him.

The celebration came to an end and everyone was exiting the reception hall. Boss and Queenie descend the stairs, waving good-bye to their guest as they made way to their limo. Boss turned to slap Tina's son Drew a five and didn't see what was coming. But Queenie did.

"Boss!" Queenie screamed.

A black Cadillac sped through the parking lot. Then the sounds of five shots rang out. All the guests ducked and screamed as they ran for cover. Wayne came out of his waist with a Glock 17 and fired shots at the Cadillac as it made its getaway.

Boss laid on the ground covered in blood with his body shielding Drew. Tina rushed past everyone, screaming, "DREW! Oh my God, Drew!" She panicked at the sight of all the blood. She snatched Drew up and quickly examined his body. Her heart calmed down some when she found nothing more than a bump on his head from the fall. "Thank God you alright." She cradled him in her arms as he cried.

Boss slowly got to his feet. Blood leaked out of him from a bullet wound in his left shoulder. "Queenie, you can get up now, they're gone." Queenie didn't move. "Queenie, baby, get up." Her body laid still. "Queenie?" Boss's heart pounded as he leaned down and turned her over. "QUEENIE!" Blood flowed from her head and chest.

"Oh God, someone call 911!" Tina screamed.

Tweety and the other guests came out of hiding and rushed over. Boss cradled her in his arms. He checked her pulse and found she still had one, but it was faint. He knew he had to get her to the hospital quick.

"Fuck an ambulance! Tina, go bring your truck around." Tina stood in shock. "Go now!" Boss demanded.

Tina ran off to retrieve her truck and rushed back to the front of the building. Boss and Wayne loaded Queenie in the backseat of Tina's Lexus truck. Wayne took Tina out of the driver's seat.

"I'll drive. You and Boss stay back there with her."

Tina wouldn't even let her boyfriend drive her truck. But considering the circumstances, she didn't bother putting up a fight. She quickly got in and Wayne peeled out of the parking lot.

Dipping through traffic with the pedal to the metal, Wayne got them to the hospital in seven minutes. The nurses rushed out, pushing a gurney. They loaded Queenie onto the stretcher then rushed her inside.

"Her pulse is fading! We have to get her in surgery right away!" the doctor yelled.

Boss tried to follow them to the back, but one of the nurses stopped him.

"Sir, you can't go back there."

"That's my wife."

"I understand, and she's in good hands." The nurse noticed a bloodstain on his shirt was getting larger. "Sir, are you injured?"

"I'll be fine."

The nurse opened his shirt anyway and took a quick look at his wound. "It looks like it was through and through. Come with me and let's get some X-rays to be sure and get you bandaged up."

Boss felt any further protest on his behalf would be useless, so he went willingly with her.

***

Boss paced the floor in the waiting room with his shoulder stitched up and arm in a sling. It'd been almost three hours that Queenie had been in surgery. Boss's worries increased with every passing minute. He felt if he stopped pacing the floor, he might fall apart.

The man that shot them was aiming for him, but Queenie jumped in front of him to protect him. The man wore a mask, but Boss had no doubt Rome was somehow behind the shooting. For that, Boss made his second vow that day. He vowed to make Rome suffer somehow more than he was suffering right behind what happened to Queenie.

Tweety walked over stood in his path forcing him to stop pacing. "Boss, baby, it's going to be alright."

Boss rested his hands on his head. "What if she don't make? Nothing is going to be alright then."

"Times like this, you got to have faith. Queenie is a fighter. She'll pull through." She rubbed her hand on his back to try and soothe him as only a mother could do.

The doctor walked into the waiting room. "Is the Bandz family out here?"

Boss came forward. "I'm Mr. Bandz, the husband. How is my wife?"

"Mr. Bandz your wife suffered a gunshot wound to the upper chest area and one to the left side of her head. The gunshot wound to her chest was through and through without any damage to any major organs or arteries.

"Well, that's good news."

"However, we weren't as lucky with the wound she suffered to the head. It damaged some nerves and part of her cerebrum. We really can't estimate the full extent of damage down at this time."

Tweety stepped forward. "Can we see her?"

"Right now, she's in an induced coma until the swelling in her brain goes down."

"Be straight with me, Doc. What is the chances of my wife pulling through?"

"Mr. Bandz, you might wanna consider calling your religious council to provide her with her last rites. Forgive me for saying, but I have to prepare you for the strong possibilities of what may be the outcome. I'm sorry, but the odds of her not making it through the night are extremely probable."

Boss felt his whole world crumbling around him. He couldn't imagine life without Queenie. The very thought ached his soul. True enough, he was her pimp and she was his hoe. But she was also his wife and he was her husband. To lose her to another pimp he could've lived with, but to lose her very presence on earth would ruin his soul. He refused to lose her.

"That's not acceptable, Doc. You do whatever you got to do to keep my wife alive. What you want, money? I got that." He pulled out racks of money from his pocket then held it out for the doctor. "Here, take it."

"Mr. Bandz, that's unnecessary."

"What, it ain't enough?" Boss rushed over to where his whores sat snatching money out of their purses and throwing it at the doctor. "If that's not enough, I got a black card. Name your fucking price and I'll pay it! Just don't let her die!"

"Mr. Bandz, this is not a matter of money. I assure you, we're doing all we can to help your wife pull through. Right now, everything boils down to her will to live. Believe me, we're doing all we can for your wife and child."

Boss looked at the doctor, frozen in confusion. "My wife and child? What child?"

The doctor returned an equal look of confusion back at him. "Mrs. Bandz is with child."

"She wanted to surprise you on the honeymoon with the news." Tina walked over and handed Boss an envelope fit for a greeting card. Boss tore it open and pulled out the greeting card. It read, "Congratulations, You're Going To Be A Father!" Inside the card was an ultrasound of the baby.

Boss nearly fell to his knees. It all felt like too much for him at once. He wanted to be happy about the baby, but there was no time for it. Not while he had to focus on keeping both his wife and child alive. He felt powerless for the first time in his life.

"I want to see my wife."

"Sure, right this way." The doctor led him to Queenie's room.

When he walked inside the sight of her threatened to burst the dams of his eyes. It was hard to believe just a few hours ago, he was looking into her beautiful smiling face. Now her head was bandaged, a plastic breathing tube was in her throat, and IV in her arm, and she was hooked up to so many machines.

The doctor put a hand of comfort on his shoulder. "The best thing you can do for her right now is pray. I'm going to leave so you can have some privacy. You can have one of the nurses page me if you need me."

"Thanks, Doc."

The doctor nodded at him and walked out, closing the door behind him.

Boss came closer to her bedside and held her hand. He planted a kiss on her lips. "I'm so sorry, baby. I should've seen it coming. This shit is all my fault. Don't you die on me, bitch. You better fight for you and our baby. I'm going to stay right here with you to make sure you do. And I promise you, Rome is going to pay for this pain."

Boss sat down in the chair next to her and stayed by her side all night.

CHAPTER 24

Tweety walked into the room and stood by Queenie's bedside. She bent down and kissed her bandaged forehead. Then she walked over to the other side of the bed, where Boss was asleep in the chair. She kissed him on the head and he awakened. "Good morning."

"Good morning, ma."

"How she's doing?"

"The same as she's been since she's been here."

Boss stretched and sat up in the chair. It'd been three days that Queenie had been fighting for hers and their unborn child's lives. Although there hadn't been any changes in her status for the better, she remained in stable condition.

"You may not see it was right now, but that's still good news. The doctors didn't think she would survive the first night. Like I told you, she's a fighter."

"I know that. What I didn't know was a few hours after saying until death do us apart, we would be faced with that scenario." Boss reached over held Queenie's hand in his.

"I understand, and we need to talk about that. If Rome is behind this, he's not going to stop until your dead."

"It's no question he's behind this. You and I both know that. That man tried to take my world from me. That's why Rome must die."

"You can't go after Rome that way just yet. You got take over the throne first."

"To hell with chasing the crown! I'm the number two pimp in the game. I'll kill that mothafucka, then there will be no choice but for the throne to mine."

"Yeah, you could do that, but you'll be no different from him. That's not respecting the game. That's not how your father would want you to gain the throne."

"I can't challenge him for the throne. He keeps hiding from me, dodging my challenges, and throwing all these goddamn obstacles in my way. Then you said yourself he's going to keep coming at me. What am I supposed to do?"

Tina and her mother Marjorie walked into the room with balloons and other items from the gift shop. Marjorie's eyes were red and swollen. She looked as if she'd been doing more crying than sleeping the past few nights. She acknowledged Tweety, then came over and hugged Boss. Her small, frail arms looked like tiny tree branches wrapped around him. She squeezed him tight, then let go and turned to Queenie.

"Any new developments in her condition?"

"Nothing new to report."

"Boss, let's go down to the cafeteria and get something to eat."

"I'm not hungry, Ma."

"Well, I am. Come on so we can give them a minute alone with her. And you and I need to finish discussing your alternative options."

Boss let go of Queenie's hand and kissed her lips. As much as he didn't want to, he left her side and followed Tweety down to the cafeteria. He was curious to what his other options could be.

***

After his conversation with his mama in the cafeteria over cheeseburgers and fries that Boss didn't touch, he went to the apartments to get cleaned up and get some rest. He couldn't go home. He'd never be able to sleep. Too many things there reminded him of Queenie. Little did he know, sleep wouldn't come so easy for him there either.

Isis was sitting at the kitchen table flipping through a *Cosmopolitan* magazine and eating a bagel when Coco walked in. Isis didn't bother looking up from her magazine. Coco rolled her eyes at her and went to the refrigerator. Not finding what she was looking for, she slammed the fridge door closed then charged up Isis. "You took my last bagel! I'm tired of you and them other greedy-ass bitches eating up my shit!"

Isis kept her head in the magazine. "Here, I only took a couple of bites of it. If it bothers you that much, you can have the rest of it." She slid the saucer with the barely-eaten bagel on it over to Coco.

Coco swiped the whole thing onto the floor. The sound of the saucer crashing to the floor breaking brought the other girls to the kitchen to see what was going on.

"Bitch, I don't want shit you had your mouth on!"

"If you don't want nothing I put my mouth on, then you must not want Boss either. Because my mouth stay on him." Isis closed her eyes, bit her lip, and moaned like she was reliving the memory of their sexcapades. She was fucking with Coco's head.

Coco picked up a cup of apple juice off the table and splashed it in her face.

Isis jumped up drenched in juice and paused a second in disbelief. Coco put her fist up, ready to fight. The kitchen got so quiet you could hear the drops of juice hit the floor. The other girls waited to see what she was going to do. Everything in her wanted to knock Coco on her ass, but she didn't want to stoop to her level. Isis started to walk off.

"Yeah, you better run, bitch. You know what it is." Coco dropped her guard.

Macita giggled. Isis stopped.

"You know what? Fuck it." She turned around and caught Coco with a right hook to the jaw, knocking spit from her mouth. She stumbled into the kitchen sink. Isis charged her. Coco tackled her into the refrigerator. knocking boxes of cereal onto the floor. Isis pushed her back, running her into Sapphire. Sapphire pushed Coco away.

"Don't touch her!" Macita yelled, then pushed Sapphire.

"Bitch!" Sapphire snatched Macita by the hair and they got to tussling.

Next thing you know, the whole house was rumbling. Tension in the house had been at an all-time high since what went down at the wedding reception. The house had been divided. Some of the girls believed Isis had something to do with what happened. The others were standing by Isis.

Boss heard the commotion going on inside before he could get his key in the door. He opened the door to a world of chaos. They were fighting all over the house. Holes were in the walls, the 72" smart TV laid on the floor with a long vertical crack in the screen, the glass center table in the front room was in pieces, and dirt from the tall plants that sat in the corner were sprawled all over the carpet. Sapphire and Macita wrestled on the floor. Coco had Isis by the hair, throwing her into the wall, the other girls were in the kitchen fighting.

Boss snatched the girls apart. "What the fuck is going on?"

"This punk-ass bitch ate my bagel!" Coco was so upset she didn't realize how petty it sounded coming out her mouth.

"Queenie's in the hospital on her death bed and you hoes fighting like cats and dogs over a bagel? A 50¢ mothafuckin' bagel? Look around this house and see how much that bagel just cost us. You petty hoes want to kill each other, go ahead. I'll replace you 50¢ bagel whores with bitches that's above such petty shit."

They hung their heads in shame and couldn't looking him in the face. Boss was going for the door to leave back out when a brick came through the picture window in the front room, shattering the glass. Afraid it might be gunshots, Kelly, Megan, and Trish, the girls Boss knocked Fleetwood for, huddled together screaming. A car could be heard peeling off in front of the house. Boss ran to the window to get a look at the car, but was too late. The car had turned the corner and vanished.

"Boss, you might want to see this."

He turned around and Isis was unwrapping a note from the brick that came through the window. He took the note from her and began reading it out loud.

"I warned you about coming for the crown. I missed you once. I won't miss again. I'ma kill everyone you love until I get you."

Boss was heated more than ever. He balled the paper up and threw it. It didn't demonstrate just how mad he was, so he snatched the brick from Isis and threw it. It made a toaster-size hole in the wall. "That's it!" He took out his phone and dialed up Rome. "You threaten my family, you put the nail in your own coffin. I'm coming for you." He ended the call and pulled out his 9mm, then treaded out the door.

"Boss, don't go after him. That's what he wants you to do." Isis and the girls tried to stop him, but he closed the door behind him and kept going.

They heard him chirp his alarm followed by his car starting up. They started cleaning up the mess around the house. A second later, a huge explosion went off in front, shaking the whole apartment building. All the girls rushed out the door to see what happened.

Flames shot up high enough to set the top of the trees near the curb on fire. Smoke engulfed the whole block. Coco was the first out the door and the first to notice it was Boss's car that blew up.

"Boss!" She tried to run to the car to see if he could still be saved. Before she could get close, another explosion went off, knocking her on her ass. The car behind his had caught fire, setting off a chain of explosions with the cars parked behind it. There was nothing any of them could do to save him.

Not long after, sirens screamed in the distance. The fire department fought to put out all the fires. First responders had the entire block blocked off. Tweety's BMW came flying through the alley. She parked in the back of the four-unit apartment building, then she and Princess raced to the front of it. The first person she saw was Macita.

"Macita, where's Boss?" Tweety lost control of her nerves and couldn't stop herself from shaking.

The sad look on Macita's face told her bad news was coming. Macita opened her mouth, but the words wouldn't come out.

Tweety grabbed her by the shirt. "Macita, where is my son!" Macita pointed at the body the coroner was wheeling towards the back of his van. "No! Lord, not my baby!"

The girls stayed behind Tweety when she ran over to the coroners demanding to see Boss's body. They denied her, and a big commotion broke out. Chief Hicks was on the scene and walked over to Tweety. He hugged her tight and felt the vibrations of her cries.

"Angela, I'm so sorry."

"Aaron, I want to see my baby."

"You can't. His body's burned so bad you wouldn't be able to recognize him. You don't need to see him like that."

"I don't care. I want to see!" He ordered the coroners to let her see. They unzipped the bag and showed her his burnt corpse. She gasped when she saw it. It was like Chief Hicks said: he was burned beyond any recognition. But she knew it was Boss by the jewelry still on it. She zipped him back up herself. The coroners proceeded to load him into the back of the van. A parade of tears came flooding down her face. The chief put his hand on her shoulder.

"Angela, I swear to you, I'm going to get whose responsible for placing that bomb in his car."

Tweety stepped back and looked him in the eye. "No need. Because now I'm finna make this mothafucka pay in the worst way."

Tweety walked off.

"Who?" She didn't answer him. "Angela! Who did this?"

She kept walking with the girls right behind her like little ducklings following Mother Goose.

"I guess it's going to take a queen to dethrone this king. So be it," she said to herself.

Rome took everything from her and now she was going to return the favor by taking away what meant the most to him: the crown...

To Be Continued...
Blood and Games 2
Coming Soon

Lock Down Publications and Ca$h Presents assisted
publishing packages.

BASIC PACKAGE $499
Editing
Cover Design
Formatting

UPGRADED PACKAGE $800
Typing
Editing
Cover Design
Formatting

ADVANCE PACKAGE $1,200
Typing
Editing
Cover Design
Formatting
Copyright registration
Proofreading
Upload book to Amazon

LDP SUPREME PACKAGE $1,500
Typing
Editing
Cover Design
Formatting
Copyright registration
Proofreading
Set up Amazon account
Upload book to Amazon
Advertise on LDP Amazon and Facebook page

***Other services available upon request. Additional charges may apply
Lock Down Publications
P.O. Box 944
Stockbridge, GA 30281-9998
Phone # 470 303-9761

Submission Guideline

Submit the first three chapters of your completed manuscript to ldpsubmissions@gmail.com, subject line: Your book's title. The manuscript must be in a .doc file and sent as an attachment. Document should be in Times New Roman, double spaced and in size 12 font. Also, provide your synopsis and full contact information. If sending multiple submissions, they must each be in a separate email.

Have a story but no way to send it electronically? You can still submit to LDP/Ca$h Presents. Send in the first three chapters, written or typed, of your completed manuscript to:

LDP: Submissions Dept
Po Box 944
Stockbridge, Ga 30281

DO NOT send original manuscript. Must be a duplicate.

Provide your synopsis and a cover letter containing your full contact information.

Thanks for considering LDP and Ca$h Presents.

<u>NEW RELEASES</u>

THE MURDER QUEENS 3 by MICHAEL GALLON

GORILLAZ IN THE TRENCHES 3 by SAYNOMORE

SALUTE MY SAVAGERY by FUMIYA PAYNE

SUPER GREMLIN by KING RIO

BLOOD AND GAMES by KING DREAM

Blood and Games

Coming Soon from Lock Down Publications/Ca$h Presents

BLOOD OF A BOSS **VI**

SHADOWS OF THE GAME II

TRAP BASTARD II

By **Askari**

LOYAL TO THE GAME **IV**

By **T.J. & Jelissa**

TRUE SAVAGE **VIII**

MIDNIGHT CARTEL IV

DOPE BOY MAGIC IV

CITY OF KINGZ III

NIGHTMARE ON SILENT AVE II

THE PLUG OF LIL MEXICO II

CLASSIC CITY II

By **Chris Green**

BLAST FOR ME **III**

A SAVAGE DOPEBOY III

CUTTHROAT MAFIA III

DUFFLE BAG CARTEL VII

HEARTLESS GOON VI

By **Ghost**

A HUSTLER'S DECEIT III

KILL ZONE II

BAE BELONGS TO ME III

TIL DEATH II

By **Aryanna**

KING OF THE TRAP III

By **T.J. Edwards**

GORILLAZ IN THE BAY V

3X KRAZY III

185

STRAIGHT BEAST MODE III

De'Kari

KINGPIN KILLAZ IV

STREET KINGS III

PAID IN BLOOD III

CARTEL KILLAZ IV

DOPE GODS III

Hood Rich

SINS OF A HUSTLA II

ASAD

YAYO V

Bred In The Game 2

S. Allen

THE STREETS WILL TALK II

By Yolanda Moore

SON OF A DOPE FIEND III

HEAVEN GOT A GHETTO III

SKI MASK MONEY III

By Renta

LOYALTY AIN'T PROMISED III

By Keith Williams

I'M NOTHING WITHOUT HIS LOVE II

SINS OF A THUG II

TO THE THUG I LOVED BEFORE II

IN A HUSTLER I TRUST II

By Monet Dragun

QUIET MONEY IV

EXTENDED CLIP III

THUG LIFE IV

By **Trai'Quan**

Blood and Games

THE STREETS MADE ME IV

By **Larry D. Wright**

IF YOU CROSS ME ONCE III

ANGEL V

By **Anthony Fields**

THE STREETS WILL NEVER CLOSE IV

By K'ajji

HARD AND RUTHLESS III

KILLA KOUNTY IV

By Khufu

MONEY GAME III

By Smoove Dolla

JACK BOYS VS DOPE BOYS IV

A GANGSTA'S QUR'AN V

COKE GIRLZ II

COKE BOYS II

LIFE OF A SAVAGE V

CHI'RAQ GANGSTAS V

SOSA GANG III

BRONX SAVAGES II

BODYMORE KINGPINS II

BLOOD OF A GOON II

By Romell Tukes

MURDA WAS THE CASE III

Elijah R. Freeman

AN UNFORESEEN LOVE IV

BABY, I'M WINTERTIME COLD III

By **Meesha**

QUEEN OF THE ZOO III

King Dream

By **Black Migo**

CONFESSIONS OF A JACKBOY III

By Nicholas Lock

KING KILLA II

By Vincent "Vitto" Holloway

BETRAYAL OF A THUG III

By Fre$h

THE BIRTH OF A GANGSTER III

By Delmont Player

TREAL LOVE II

By Le'Monica Jackson

FOR THE LOVE OF BLOOD III

By Jamel Mitchell

RAN OFF ON DA PLUG II

By Paper Boi Rari

HOOD CONSIGLIERE III

By Keese

PRETTY GIRLS DO NASTY THINGS II

By Nicole Goosby

LOVE IN THE TRENCHES II

By Corey Robinson

IT'S JUST ME AND YOU II

By Ah'Million

FOREVER GANGSTA III

By Adrian Dulan

THE COCAINE PRINCESS IX

SUPER GREMLIN II

By King Rio

CRIME BOSS II

Playa Ray

Blood and Games

LOYALTY IS EVERYTHING III
Molotti
HERE TODAY GONE TOMORROW II
By Fly Rock
REAL G'S MOVE IN SILENCE II
By Von Diesel
GRIMEY WAYS IV
By Ray Vinci
SALUTE MY SAVAGERY II
By Fumiya Payne
BLOOD AND GAMES II
By King Dream

Available Now

RESTRAINING ORDER **I & II**
By **CA$H & Coffee**
LOVE KNOWS NO BOUNDARIES **I II & III**
By **Coffee**
RAISED AS A GOON I, II, III & IV
BRED BY THE SLUMS I, II, III
BLAST FOR ME I & II
ROTTEN TO THE CORE I II III
A BRONX TALE I, II, III
DUFFLE BAG CARTEL I II III IV V VI
HEARTLESS GOON I II III IV V

King Dream

A SAVAGE DOPEBOY I II
DRUG LORDS I II III
CUTTHROAT MAFIA I II
KING OF THE TRENCHES
By **Ghost**
LAY IT DOWN **I & II**
LAST OF A DYING BREED I II
BLOOD STAINS OF A SHOTTA I & II III
By **Jamaica**
LOYAL TO THE GAME I II III
LIFE OF SIN I, II III
By **TJ & Jelissa**
BLOODY COMMAS I & II
SKI MASK CARTEL I II & III
KING OF NEW YORK I II,III IV V
RISE TO POWER I II III
COKE KINGS I II III IV V
BORN HEARTLESS I II III IV
KING OF THE TRAP I II
By **T.J. Edwards**
IF LOVING HIM IS WRONG…I & II
LOVE ME EVEN WHEN IT HURTS I II III
By **Jelissa**
WHEN THE STREETS CLAP BACK I & II III
THE HEART OF A SAVAGE I II III IV
MONEY MAFIA I II
LOYAL TO THE SOIL I II III
By **Jibril Williams**
A DISTINGUISHED THUG STOLE MY HEART I II & III
LOVE SHOULDN'T HURT I II III IV

Blood and Games

RENEGADE BOYS I II III IV

PAID IN KARMA I II III

SAVAGE STORMS I II III

AN UNFORESEEN LOVE I II III

BABY, I'M WINTERTIME COLD I II

By **Meesha**

A GANGSTER'S CODE I &, II III

A GANGSTER'S SYN I II III

THE SAVAGE LIFE I II III

CHAINED TO THE STREETS I II III

BLOOD ON THE MONEY I II III

A GANGSTA'S PAIN I II III

By J-Blunt

PUSH IT TO THE LIMIT

By **Bre' Hayes**

BLOOD OF A BOSS **I, II, III, IV, V**

SHADOWS OF THE GAME

TRAP BASTARD

By **Askari**

THE STREETS BLEED MURDER **I, II & III**

THE HEART OF A GANGSTA I II& III

By **Jerry Jackson**

CUM FOR ME I II III IV V VI VII VIII

An **LDP Erotica Collaboration**

BRIDE OF A HUSTLA **I II & II**

THE FETTI GIRLS **I, II& III**

CORRUPTED BY A GANGSTA I, II III, IV

BLINDED BY HIS LOVE

THE PRICE YOU PAY FOR LOVE I, II ,III

DOPE GIRL MAGIC I II III

King Dream

By **Destiny Skai**
WHEN A GOOD GIRL GOES BAD
By **Adrienne**
THE COST OF LOYALTY I II III
By Kweli
A GANGSTER'S REVENGE **I II III & IV**
THE BOSS MAN'S DAUGHTERS I II III IV V
A SAVAGE LOVE **I & II**
BAE BELONGS TO ME I II
A HUSTLER'S DECEIT I, II, III
WHAT BAD BITCHES DO I, II, III
SOUL OF A MONSTER I II III
KILL ZONE
A DOPE BOY'S QUEEN I II III
TIL DEATH
By **Aryanna**
A KINGPIN'S AMBITON
A KINGPIN'S AMBITION **II**
I MURDER FOR THE DOUGH
By **Ambitious**
TRUE SAVAGE I II III IV V VI VII
DOPE BOY MAGIC I, II, III
MIDNIGHT CARTEL I II III
CITY OF KINGZ I II
NIGHTMARE ON SILENT AVE
THE PLUG OF LIL MEXICO II
CLASSIC CITY
By **Chris Green**
A DOPEBOY'S PRAYER
By **Eddie "Wolf" Lee**

Blood and Games

THE KING CARTEL **I, II & III**

By **Frank Gresham**

THESE NIGGAS AIN'T LOYAL **I, II & III**

By **Nikki Tee**

GANGSTA SHYT **I II &III**

By **CATO**

THE ULTIMATE BETRAYAL

By **Phoenix**

BOSS'N UP **I , II & III**

By **Royal Nicole**

I LOVE YOU TO DEATH

By **Destiny J**

I RIDE FOR MY HITTA

I STILL RIDE FOR MY HITTA

By **Misty Holt**

LOVE & CHASIN' PAPER

By **Qay Crockett**

TO DIE IN VAIN

SINS OF A HUSTLA

By **ASAD**

BROOKLYN HUSTLAZ

By **Boogsy Morina**

BROOKLYN ON LOCK I & II

By **Sonovia**

GANGSTA CITY

By **Teddy Duke**

A DRUG KING AND HIS DIAMOND I & II III

A DOPEMAN'S RICHES

HER MAN, MINE'S TOO I, II

CASH MONEY HO'S

King Dream

THE WIFEY I USED TO BE I II
PRETTY GIRLS DO NASTY THINGS
By Nicole Goosby
TRAPHOUSE KING **I II & III**
KINGPIN KILLAZ I II III
STREET KINGS I II
PAID IN BLOOD **I II**
CARTEL KILLAZ I II III
DOPE GODS I II
By **Hood Rich**
LIPSTICK KILLAH **I, II, III**
CRIME OF PASSION I II & III
FRIEND OR FOE I II III
By **Mimi**
STEADY MOBBN' **I, II, III**
THE STREETS STAINED MY SOUL I II III
By **Marcellus Allen**
WHO SHOT YA **I, II, III**
SON OF A DOPE FIEND I II
HEAVEN GOT A GHETTO I II
SKI MASK MONEY I II
Renta
GORILLAZ IN THE BAY **I II III IV**
TEARS OF A GANGSTA I II
3X KRAZY I II
STRAIGHT BEAST MODE I II
DE'KARI
TRIGGADALE I II III
MURDAROBER WAS THE CASE I II
Elijah R. Freeman

Blood and Games

GOD BLESS THE TRAPPERS I, II, III
THESE SCANDALOUS STREETS I, II, III
FEAR MY GANGSTA I, II, III IV, V
THESE STREETS DON'T LOVE NOBODY I, II
BURY ME A G I, II, III, IV, V
A GANGSTA'S EMPIRE I, II, III, IV
THE DOPEMAN'S BODYGAURD I II
THE REALEST KILLAZ I II III
THE LAST OF THE OGS I II III
Tranay Adams
THE STREETS ARE CALLING
Duquie Wilson
MARRIED TO A BOSS I II III
By Destiny Skai & Chris Green
KINGZ OF THE GAME I II III IV V VI VII
CRIME BOSS
Playa Ray
SLAUGHTER GANG I II III
RUTHLESS HEART I II III
By Willie Slaughter
FUK SHYT
By Blakk Diamond
DON'T F#CK WITH MY HEART I II
By Linnea
ADDICTED TO THE DRAMA I II III
IN THE ARM OF HIS BOSS II
By Jamila
YAYO I II III IV
A SHOOTER'S AMBITION I II
BRED IN THE GAME

King Dream

By S. Allen

TRAP GOD I II III

RICH $AVAGE I II III

MONEY IN THE GRAVE I II III

By Martell Troublesome Bolden

FOREVER GANGSTA I II

GLOCKS ON SATIN SHEETS I II

By Adrian Dulan

TOE TAGZ I II III IV

LEVELS TO THIS SHYT I II

IT'S JUST ME AND YOU

By Ah'Million

KINGPIN DREAMS I II III

RAN OFF ON DA PLUG

By Paper Boi Rari

CONFESSIONS OF A GANGSTA I II III IV

CONFESSIONS OF A JACKBOY I II

By Nicholas Lock

I'M NOTHING WITHOUT HIS LOVE

SINS OF A THUG

TO THE THUG I LOVED BEFORE

A GANGSTA SAVED XMAS

IN A HUSTLER I TRUST

By Monet Dragun

CAUGHT UP IN THE LIFE I II III

THE STREETS NEVER LET GO I II III

By Robert Baptiste

NEW TO THE GAME I II III

MONEY, MURDER & MEMORIES I II III

By **Malik D. Rice**

Blood and Games

LIFE OF A SAVAGE I II III IV

A GANGSTA'S QUR'AN I II III IV

MURDA SEASON I II III

GANGLAND CARTEL I II III

CHI'RAQ GANGSTAS I II III IV

KILLERS ON ELM STREET I II III

JACK BOYZ N DA BRONX I II III

A DOPEBOY'S DREAM I II III

JACK BOYS VS DOPE BOYS I II III

COKE GIRLZ

COKE BOYS

SOSA GANG I II

BRONX SAVAGES

BODYMORE KINGPINS

BLOOD OF A GOON

By Romell Tukes

LOYALTY AIN'T PROMISED I II

By Keith Williams

QUIET MONEY I II III

THUG LIFE I II III

EXTENDED CLIP I II

A GANGSTA'S PARADISE

By **Trai'Quan**

THE STREETS MADE ME I II III

By **Larry D. Wright**

THE ULTIMATE SACRIFICE I, II, III, IV, V, VI

KHADIFI

IF YOU CROSS ME ONCE I II

ANGEL I II III IV

IN THE BLINK OF AN EYE

King Dream

By **Anthony Fields**

THE LIFE OF A HOOD STAR

By **Ca$h & Rashia Wilson**

THE STREETS WILL NEVER CLOSE I II III

By **K'ajji**

CREAM I II III

THE STREETS WILL TALK

By **Yolanda Moore**

NIGHTMARES OF A HUSTLA I II III

BLOOD AND GAMES

By **King Dream**

CONCRETE KILLA I II III

VICIOUS LOYALTY I II III

By **Kingpen**

HARD AND RUTHLESS I II

MOB TOWN 251

THE BILLIONAIRE BENTLEYS I II III

REAL G'S MOVE IN SILENCE

By **Von Diesel**

GHOST MOB

Stilloan Robinson

MOB TIES I II III IV V VI

SOUL OF A HUSTLER, HEART OF A KILLER I II

GORILLAZ IN THE TRENCHES I II III

By **SayNoMore**

BODYMORE MURDERLAND I II III

THE BIRTH OF A GANGSTER I II

By **Delmont Player**

FOR THE LOVE OF A BOSS

By **C. D. Blue**

Blood and Games

MOBBED UP I II III IV

THE BRICK MAN I II III IV V

THE COCAINE PRINCESS I II III IV V VI VII VIII

SUPER GREMLIN

By King Rio

KILLA KOUNTY I II III IV

By Khufu

MONEY GAME I II

By Smoove Dolla

A GANGSTA'S KARMA I II III

By FLAME

KING OF THE TRENCHES I II III

by **GHOST & TRANAY ADAMS**

QUEEN OF THE ZOO I II

By **Black Migo**

GRIMEY WAYS I II III

By Ray Vinci

XMAS WITH AN ATL SHOOTER

By Ca$h & Destiny Skai

KING KILLA

By Vincent "Vitto" Holloway

BETRAYAL OF A THUG I II

By Fre$h

THE MURDER QUEENS I II III

By Michael Gallon

TREAL LOVE

By Le'Monica Jackson

FOR THE LOVE OF BLOOD I II

By Jamel Mitchell

HOOD CONSIGLIERE I II

King Dream

By Keese

PROTÉGÉ OF A LEGEND I II III

LOVE IN THE TRENCHES

By Corey Robinson

BORN IN THE GRAVE I II III

By Self Made Tay

MOAN IN MY MOUTH

By XTASY

TORN BETWEEN A GANGSTER AND A GENTLEMAN

By J-BLUNT & Miss Kim

LOYALTY IS EVERYTHING I II

Molotti

HERE TODAY GONE TOMORROW

By Fly Rock

PILLOW PRINCESS

By S. Hawkins

NAÏVE TO THE STREETS

WOMEN LIE MEN LIE I II III

GIRLS FALL LIKE DOMINOS

STACK BEFORE YOU SPURLGE

FIFTY SHADES OF SNOW I II III

By A. Roy Milligan

SALUTE MY SAVAGERY

By Fumiya Payne

BOOKS BY LDP'S CEO, CA$H

TRUST IN NO MAN

TRUST IN NO MAN 2

TRUST IN NO MAN 3

BONDED BY BLOOD

SHORTY GOT A THUG

THUGS CRY

THUGS CRY 2

THUGS CRY 3

TRUST NO BITCH

TRUST NO BITCH 2

TRUST NO BITCH 3

TIL MY CASKET DROPS

RESTRAINING ORDER

RESTRAINING ORDER 2

IN LOVE WITH A CONVICT

LIFE OF A HOOD STAR

XMAS WITH AN ATL SHOOTER

King Dream